WHITE LINES
&
LOT LIZARDS

by Larry Murley
Illustrated by Kerry Kelly

Dedicated to

Bill Carlson

I first met Bill in 1985 or '86 when I was teaching truck driving in Denver. He went through my course and graduated. Some months afterward, when I went back on the road, Bill went to work for the same company. Bill was a Vietnam Vet suffering from illnesses resulting from Agent Orange. He was getting quiet ill when I lost contact with him in about '92.

So straighten up Bill! If you are still alive and kicking, this is for you! And all those other Vets that found a home behind the wheel of an 18-wheeler.

www.larrymurley.com
www.facebook.com/WhiteLinesandLotLizards

Foreword

This story, about Evan Smith, I think will find a home in the hearts of many Veterans. I myself found I had great difficulty with working in the system after coming back from Vietnam. It took me several years to find myself behind the wheel of a "large car, but once I did, I found myself at home. No more people looking over my shoulder, the ability to think and act for myself. I also rode motorcycles for a number of years. You watch your motorcycle riders and you will find many vets holding those handlebars, and allowing memories to slide by like the wind. So, enjoy this tale, and see if you find anyone that you might know, or have known, between the pages of this book. Oh, yeah, keep it out of the hands of little children. It was never meant for them.

The snow was coming down hard now. I could see the lights of Billings, Montana coming up just ahead the welcoming neon of the Pilot Truck Stop on the left. Fuck yeah, it's time for a shower and food. It had been snowing ever since we came thru the Windy, just slicker than shit all the way across South Dakota. Didn't appear to be much relief in sight, either.

I reached up and hit the little buzzer that would wake up my co-driver 'Shadow' so she could get her gorgeous face together before we step out of the large car. Yeah, and so she could put some clothes on, too. She had just slid out of the sleeper into the seat next to me, butt naked. That just always made my attitude go up when she did that. Along with everything else.

I eased the Pete passed the entrance to the Pilot and down the rows of Stainless Steel Stallions parked neatly in order. That always amazed me, seeing how most of them were driven by people that didn't just always like to follow rules. Just as we reached the back side of the truck stop building a full grown Montana Bear stepped out from the building and raised his arm for me to stop. What the fuck did I do? I rolled the window down.

"Hey, Driver, which way did you come from?"

"The dirty side" I answered.

He grinned. "Well, find you a comfortable spot back there. We are shutting the west bound side down for the night. Already had a bunch of accidents up there."

I answered, "Well, my dispatcher is gonna hate

your ass, but don't worry about it. He hates every body's ass. Me, I love ya for it. I've had enough of this shit for today."

I found a spot for the Pete and the trailer load of books from Barnes & Nobel. At least we didn't have a load of "hot freight" this time. These books will be good when they get there. Shadow and I put on our jackets and hats then opened the door and stepped out into the Montana blizzard. BRRRRR! We hurried inside.

It was warm in the building. Music was playing on the truck stops sound system. Some slow cowboy ballad, about his lost girl. We hit the restrooms first and washed up. I was standing watching a couple of drivers playing video games, trying to understand why they liked that shit. Just totally failed.

Shadow came up behind me and nudged me, "Hey, I'm hungry!"

I nodded, "Me too."

We walked through to the restaurant, found a booth and slid in, taking off our jackets and hats and stowing them on the seat and table next to the window. The wind was blowing the snow against the window and it was starting to stick in places and giving the place an aura of security from the storm. The worn out looking waitress came and tossed us a menu on the table and asked what we wanted to drink. I answered tea, and Shadow wanted coffee. We watched out the window as the lights from more big rigs came across the overpass, seeking refuge from the storm. We ate our dinner in silence, and smoked a cigarette. I noticed the tables were filling up and more people were coming in. I looked at Shadow.

"We better get outta here. They are going to need the tables."

She nodded ok. We grabbed out jackets and hats, and headed for our truck.

It was warm and comfortable in the Pete when we climbed in the cab. Shadow went straight to rolling a joint. I turned on our small TV just in time to catch the late night weather. It didn't look good, but the system was supposed to pass us by morning. I took the joint from her when it was handed to me. I took a long hit, held it for a few seconds, then cracked a window and blew the smoke out. Shadow duplicated the action on her side of the truck. I put a Blue Oyster Cult tape in the player, cranked it up just a bit and settled back in the air seat. The cascade of snowflakes blowing in the wind seemed to rise and fall with the music. I looked to my right. Shadow had come out of her clothes and was sitting naked there beside me smoking a cigarette and zoning out on the music. Slowly she traced the circle of her left nipple with her finger tip......

Our alarm went off at seven am. We grabbed our shower bags and stepped out into the deep snow of the truck stop. We didn't need fuel so we paid our five bucks each for the shower. We hurried back to Shower Room #4, went inside, stripped and stepped into the shower together. I soaped her back and she soaped mine. Then I soaped her breasts. She smiled and said it isn't as much fun soaping a guy's chest. I agreed. We had sex together occasionally, but not regularly. She was a knockout I thought. But we made a great team. I trusted her driving, she took care of the truck, inside and out, and she helped with loading and unloading. We liked the same kind of music, we never quarreled. She was fun to be with. Oh, and it was fun to see jaws drop when she appeared. Every driver out there had a line trying to pick her up, but she would just smile. You see, Shadow really preferred girls.

After showers and breakfast, we checked at the fuel desk and found that HP had opened the road with single lane traffic on both sides. I took the jump seat this time. Shadow got behind the wheel and adjusted the seat and mirrors and whatever to fit her. She put the Pete in gear and released the parking brake. The Pete eased forward. It spun a few times, then found traction. When we turned westbound on I-90, I heaved a bit of a sigh of relief. We would only be a day late. Not too bad, considering the conditions.

It took us all day to reach Spokane. The warehouse was open 24 hours, so I backed our wagon into the dock. Shadow was already in the bunk I stood and watched the fork lift trucks emptying the forty eight foot, hundred two inch wide reefer. When they were done I closed the doors, picked up my signed bills and climbed up in the Pete and drove out to a truck stop. I went in and found myself a phone at one of the tables in restaurant and called my dispatcher. I told him my little wagon was empty. He informed me that a load of frozen corn was waiting on me about a hundred miles south. Oh well, I didn't want to sleep anyway.

As I left the Interstate heading down the skinny road southbound, it was apparent that the snowplows had not done a super job. Snow was about 2 or 3 inches deep and it was kinda greasy. Definitely not a "haul ass" day. I was able to hold the speedometer at about 50, except on some of the curves. As a result, about two and a half hours later I was backing the wagon into a dock at a produce facility. I went inside and sized up the load and supervised the placement of the pallets of cut corn, trying to balance the weight, so that I wouldn't be too heavy on my drive axles. Evidently I did a good job, for when I rolled across the scales, I was just a shade light of 36,000 on both truck and trailer, and my fuel tanks were sitting at 3/4 full. The load was headed for the Safeway warehouse in Denver and was already late due to everyone, including me, having to navigate a nasty blizzard.

I headed on south for Pasco and the Columbia River, best of all, an Interstate Highway, I-84. It would be a relief to get off the skinny roads and back on the big road. I was able to kick it up another 10 mph with a full load holding me down, and a few hours later we were crossing the bridge over the river into Oregon. About that time, Shadow woke up. OK, I need to stop calling her Shadow. Her real name was Sheryl.

So Sheryl came forward and sat down beside me, saying, "Well, I guess we got another load."

"Yep. Headed for Denver. Need to be there yesterday."

"Figures," she said. "Nothing new about that."

I glanced down at the big river. It had something

of a majesty to it. I had seen it for the first time about 16 or 17 years ago before I started driving. A lot had happened in that time, a whole lot had happened.

"So, when is it time for me to be pilot of this aircraft?" Sheryl asked.

"Oh, I don't know. I'm doing ok. How about if I take you up over Cabbage and The Blues, and hand it off to you at the truck stop at La Grande, just before we get to Idaho?"

"Sounds good to me. So, I think it is attitude adjustment time!"

"OK, but I am gonna pass for now and see if we have to chain up for Cabbage."

Sheryl reached back and pulled a joint she had already rolled and lit it. The smell filled the cab. She quickly rolled the window down and let it clear. We were real careful of leaving the smell in the cab, and always kept fragrance sprayers in the truck to cover it.

Before we reached Pendleton I could see the

flashing lights at the chain area. Yep, it's chain-up time in Oregon.

I pulled in right at the entrance and found myself a spot. I climbed out into the biting cold, pulling on my coat, hat and gloves. I pulled the chains off the hangers on the frame of the Pete, and dropped the set of doubles over the rear drivers and rolled the Pete back into them. I got out and hooked them up and put the tensioners into place. I got back in and drove to the other end of the chain area, got out and tightened everything again. By then, my fingers had no feeling. I climbed back in, took off my coat and hat and gloves, kicked the snow off my boots and flipped the heater blower on high. I just sat there and soaked up heat.

After trudging up Cabbage in heavy snow and wading all the way across The Blues, we came down off the mountain. The Idaho snowplows were out in force. Plus the sun came out and rendered a bit of aid to them.

We pulled onto the fuel Islands and filled both tanks, taking on about a hundred and seventy-five gallons. I paid for it at the desk, then joined Sheryl in the restaurant.

They had the dinner time buffet on special, so we went for the salad bar first, following it with fried chicken, mashed potatoes and gravy. Add some veggies, and piece of coconut crème pie. I looked at Sheryl.

"Now you have to drive, I can't fit behind the wheel!"

She looked at me and said "Yessuh Massah!"

We hit the road again, scootin' our little wagon of corn toward the Mile High. After digesting a spell I went to bed. It had been a long day. Hell, it had been a long several days.

When I woke, we were just rolling into Rock Springs, Wyoming. It was daylight. I looked at my watch, it was 8:30. I slid into my jeans and sat down in the jump seat as Sheryl maneuvered the big truck into a lane and up to the fuel pumps.

"Wow, babe, that was one good rest! About 12 hours worth looks like. Did you do all right?"

"Yeah, I had to show a little tit and smile seductively at the chicken-house operator as we came into Wyoming. He said I was out of hours, but he decided it would be ok if I drove on up here."

We topped off the tanks and took a shower, had breakfast, then I headed the Pete in an easterly direction.

I had been down this highway many times, but today I couldn't help but remember the first time on the Harley. That week had changed the course of my life. Sheryl had crawled into bed and I was lost in my thoughts as I rolled across the Wyoming wastelands. They have their own beauty, but the size and distance gnaws on you, as you watch the white lines disappear under the nose of the Pete. Thoughts of the summer of 1970 came rushing back. Before long I was hanging a left on Old US 287, heading towards Fort Collins. Memories of a chilly evening filled my mind as I came down past the little store and restaurant at Livermore known as The Forks. I had to drop one gear before I reached the Peak, but had put it back into the big hole before I flashed by the sign that said Owl Canyon Road. On the straightaway past Haystack Rock it had gotten dark, just like it had that evening 16, no, 17 years ago. But it still was fresh in my mind. I eased off the throttle and rounded the curve at Ted's Place, then took a right turn onto the old road that went through the little town of La Porte. I saw a spot in front of Vern's Restaurant and pulled in, barely off the road. I left my flashers on.

Sheryl had joined me, dressed this time.

"Where are we?"

"Come on. You are going to take a walk down memory lane with me."

"Ok" she smiled and followed me into the cafe.

As we entered she looked around and said, "Damn, that's a lot of dead animals!"

"Uh huh."

We sat and ordered dinner. I broke the silence.
"Sheryl, have I ever told you how my truck driving career started?"

"No, but I would be interested."

"Well, it all started way back in 1970, right after I came back from Vietnam. It's kinda long, but we have only another hour to our destination."

So here is the story I told her that evening.

I had spent two tours in Vietnam, and had returned home for the most part in one piece. True, I did have ear fungus and toe fungus and other skin problems as a result of my time in the jungle. I also had a severe mistrust of anyone in authority. Not to say I didn't respect authority, I just was real leery of those figures till I got to know them. I didn't like to be in large crowds either, to a point that if I wanted to go see a movie I would pick times that a theater would be nearly empty. And then there were the dreams.

I had come home with a pretty good size chunk of change. I didn't gamble, wasn't much of a drinker, and although those pretty Vietnamese girls were enticing, I knew sometimes those delicious little bodies contained lethal diseases. Now, don't get me wrong, I did partake a few times, but I was selective and careful.

I got a job in a machine shop right off. I had always enjoyed making things and building stuff, and I might have stayed there, but this little foreman whose dad owned the place came up one afternoon and stuck his bearded blond face with his little round glasses in front of me and said, "Hey, Smith, did you get tired of killing babies for The Man?"

I hit him. I hit him so hard that his hard hat went all the way into the next room. I was on top of him, planning on finishing the job, when a couple of guys lifted me off and were talking to me. I slowly came back to the present. It had been only a day or two since I had gotten my last check, but I didn't even go to the office. I just left my hardhat and company tools and left. It took me several hours that evening to calm my self down telling myself, hey man, you can't do that stuff. It won't get you anywhere.

I went out the next morning to find another job. Turns out it took me a couple of days, but I found a job framing houses, and it was satisfying enough. It was hard physical work, but I kinda like that sorta thing. And I met this girl, Sam - short for Samantha - she and I were attracted to each other from the first. I didn't want a relationship. I had to much in my own head that I had to sort out, and she didn't either. She was kinda hippy-ish. You know, free love and that sort of thing. We were all over each others bodies for a couple of months or so. She was blonde and loved to dance, and was plain just fun to be with.

One evening I came home, showered and ate and crawled in bed and let my tired muscles stretch and relax. I guess I kinda dozed. I awoke when something touched me and I reacted. I was back in the jungle, I twisted the body under me and was preparing a jab to the windpipe when a voice said

"No, no, Evan, it's me, Sam!"

That brought me back to reality. I rolled off her.

"Sam, I am so sorry! I should have told you never touch me or move me when I'm asleep. Always call out to me, or shake the bed!"

I lay back and calmed myself. She slipped out of her clothes and climbed on top of me and sat astride me. I looked up at her beautiful tanned body with firm hard breasts that were not large, but not small either. Her nipples pointed straight out, and I had found out first hand that they were quite tasty.

"Now, Mr. Evan, I am going to make you pay for

attempting to murder your only girl friend" she murmured as she leaned forward and kissed my neck and shoulders, rubbing those hard little nipples on my chest.

She rocked her hips back and forth, grinding her sweet bush into my manhood. I shifted so that something could make entry, but she would have none of that. She slid down away from me, and kissed and explored my chest and abdomen with her lips and tongue, occasionally nipping me with her teeth. Down and down she went, down the inside of my thigh, then across to the other thigh. I could feel her breasts on each side of my leg on her way up. Then she was rubbing her pussy on the top of my foot and up my leg. You can imagine by now that I had a raging erection.

As she moved back up my leg she stopped. She arched her back, then she dropped her head, taking the entire length of my shaft into her mouth. She slowly pulled her mouth back. I raised my head. She rolled her tongue around the head of my dick, taking only a small part of it into her mouth as she smiled at me. A sweet ,sexy, almost innocent smile, then slowly back all the way into her mouth. I moaned and dropped back to my pillow. She was just about to get rewarded for her efforts, but she knew, and she stopped. She slid up my body , then lowered herself down to my erect member. Oh. My. God. Not that the deity had anything to do with that moment. She started a slow rocking movement as if she was riding a horse at a slow canter. It was driving me insane!

I raised up and took her into my arms. Our lips met, our tongues played tag with each other, our breaths came in unison. I looked at the beautiful face, sublime in ecstasy. I was surprised to find tears running down her cheeks. Then, as if choreographed, our passion exploded together.

We held each other quietly, still sitting up in bed. Then finally we crumpled to our sides, still in each others arms, our faces touching. We slept.

We awoke several hours later. We lay back and smoked a cigarette. She sighed, and shifted her body facing me.

"Now comes the hard part, Evan. I am leaving."

I sat up quickly and looked at her.

"I hate this. I really care for you, but the chance of a lifetime has just opened up for me, and it takes me far away. I have a chance to go study under this famous professor in Egypt and work at the digs around the pyramids. I've dreamed about this my whole life."

"Sam, you don't have to apologize to me. I am quite fond of you as well. But, if I have learned anything, you must follow your dreams. I have watched a lot of young men lose their chance at a life. To begrudge you this opportunity, no. Go for it sweetheart."

"Evan, you are the best! Can we write and stay in touch, please?" I nodded yes.

We spent the rest of the night cuddling, kissing, talking, and just feeling that great feeling of being with a person that you care about. I had not had many in my life. I would sorely miss Sam.

We said our goodbyes the next morning. After she left, and I went down to the housing project where I was working. Days went by. I was almost getting comfortable until the joker messed it up. Every job has one, and this one was a redneck kid whose favorite expression was "Hey, watch this!"

You know the type.

Well, I was sheeting this roof and I was setting the bottom sheet, nailing the bottom to the rafter when Smart Ass slipped up behind me and grabbed me and yelled

"Watch out, Smith!"

I am not sure what I did, but I threw him over my head and off the roof. I guess God watches out for the stupid people, cause somehow I threw him into a big pile of sand and didn't hurt him too bad. But I got fired anyway.

I was on my way home, kinda feeling sorry for myself, when I glance over to my right and there was this absolutely beautiful silver Harley Davidson Motorcycle. I couldn't take my eyes off it. I drove by, then made a u-turn in the middle of the block and came back and pulled into a parking place beside it.

It was a small dealership, with other bikes parked along the sidewalk, but none like the silver one. I stepped out of the truck and walked around the bike. It wasn't new, but it was hard to tell. The chrome and the paint was brightly polished, no leaks were evident on the sidewalk under it. Both tires seemed new, and the chain was well oiled. It showed no wear. I was under it's spell, and it was talking to me so loud that I jumped when some one said

"It's a beauty, isn't it?"

I answered, "Yep, it is. How much?"

"Well, it's on consignment. The folks are inside, we just unloaded it. Let's go see."

I followed him inside, a couple both in their mid-forties were talking with another guy. My guy interrupted.

"How much do want for the bike? This young man is interested."

The couple turned. The woman gasped slightly.

"You look so much like my Jimmie! It was his bike, he got it just before he went to Vietnam." She wiped her eyes.

I dropped my head. "I am so sorry for your loss, I just finished my second tour a few months ago. I lost a lot of good friends."

The lady dabbed her eyes and turned to her husband.

"James, let's go next door to the Cafe and buy this young man lunch. I want to talk with him." And with we were off to lunch.

We seated ourselves in a booth in the small cafe and after the waitress had taken our order, we started to talk about Vietnam and the where's, when's, and what-for's. She asked me why I had gone back the second time. I basically told her that I had made friends there and felt a responsibility to some of them. I really had no where else to go at the time. I found out Jimmie was their only child and they both had taken it pretty hard for several months. It had finally gotten too difficult to look at the bike in the garage every time they walked past it and they had decided to sell it. They told me what Jimmie had paid for the bike. It was a good price. I told them I would be willing to pay that for it. We talked for a while longer, then went back to the dealership and they helped us with the transfer of ownership and license applications. I wrote them a check and handed it over to them. The lady took the check, then quickly hugged me and sobbed just ever so softly on my shoulder, then turned quickly and they were gone.

I told the salesman I had first talked to that I would return the next day and pick up the bike if they would check it out. He agreed.

That night I lay in bed and thought about my life. It seemed clear that I wasn't well suited for working with groups of people, under supervision. I thought about the bike. It had been a complete impulse. I had never even thought buying a big road bike, not ever. I had always enjoyed riding mostly Yamaha's and Honda's, a Triumph once or twice. I looked around the small apartment that suddenly seemed confining. I had been 15,000 miles from home, but knew little about America. I had some money left. maybe I would just go explore, instead of getting another job for a while. Yeah, that would work. I drifted off to sleep, with visions of white lines reaching into oblivion in front of me.

I arose next morning with a feeling of excitement

that was new to me. I hopped into my truck and drove down to the used car lot I had bought it from. The guy that I had bought it from stepped out of his office.

"Hey, Evan. What can I do for you?"

"Buy my truck back."

"What's the matter with it?"

"Nothing, it's a good truck. I am leaving town. Have no place to leave it."

We went inside and after dickering a few minutes he wound up buying it back for $300 less than I paid for it. I was happy with that. I took my little wad of cash and walked back to the bike shop. The Harley was sitting on the sidewalk, looking good. The salesman came out and told me they had adjusted the chain, changed oil, and checked the tire air pressure. It was ready to roll. I paid them for their services.

I walked around in their store. I picked me out a sleeping bag, a helmet, goggles, a few other items I felt might come in handy. I strapped the bag on behind the seat, making a nice back support for me, and donned my new helmet and glasses. I threw my leg over, set the bike up and kicked the stand up. I started it up. It purred. I dropped it into gear and rolled out into the street. I turned on Main Street, went down to the light, and turned left onto US67. The sign said Dallas, 167 miles.

Much later

I had spent the weekend in Phoenix ridding with some old Nam buddies of mine. We went up to Prescott and over to Flagstaff, then down to the Verde River. Someone suggested we ride over to Verde Hot Springs. It was a hot, dusty ride, but when we finally arrived. We found the place covered with hippies, but they seemed like a cool bunch, so we set us up a camp and built a campfire as it was getting a bit late when we got there. We roasted a package of hotdogs on the fire and I ate a couple and washed them down with a cold Pepsi. It was a hot night, so I walked down to the little beach there on the edge of the river, stripped off my clothes and waded in. The water was cool and refreshing. I swam upstream a bit, then floated back down, and got out and got dressed. Verde Hot Springs was the site of a hotel and a spa back in the

30's. Even in the 60's some of the walls still existed. They were made of round volcanic rock cemented together. I sat on the bank in the moonlight trying to envision what it must of looked like. The bath houses were still there, in bad repair. I wasn't about to try them out at night, too many scorpions and rattlesnakes. About that time, a voice beside me said

"Hey, stranger, you look lonely and deep in thought."

I looked up to see a cute little redheaded girl, couldn't have been more than sixteen, standing beside me butt naked. I stood up quickly.

"Young lady, you shouldn't be running around like that. How old are you?"

"Sixteen. And why not? One should be free of clothes in a place like this."

"Well, are your parents here? Someone responsible for you?"

"Nope. They are back in Wisconsin, stuck in their narrow little world. Nope. Just me and my old man."

About that time this skinny kid with a feeble attempt at a beard and mustache walks out of the trees, dressed the same way she was. He was all of seventeen or eighteen, and was evidently tripping on something.

"Hey, Sunshine, where'd ya go? Wha'cha doin' with this dude?" I answered for her.

"She is doing nothing with this dude, just talking. Boy, you are all fucked up, what are you on?"

"Oh, man, I scored some really fine Purple Haze. This so cool."

Sunshine answered with "You didn't save any for me?"

He said, "Aw, no, man!" and walked off into the river.

I told her she better go get the little fart before he drowned himself, and turned and went back to my bedroll and crashed for the night, fairly disgusted with the flower generation.

Next morning I grabbed a towel and headed for one of the bathhouses. On the way there were a couple of hippie girls sunbathing on sections of the old foundations and walls, and one sitting cross legged on a piece of concrete naked meditating toward the rising sun. I went into the room and checked for unwanted visitors of the poisonous variety, and then lowered myself into the hot water. Ahhhh, I could get used to this. I made a mental note to keep an eye out for hot springs in my travels.

I sat there for sometime soaking and relaxing. Finally, the door opened and in came the little redhead from last night, without asking, and she was still naked and dirty. She stepped down into the tub.

"Hey," I said, "don't you ever ask for permission before you invade someone's space?" She only smiled. I realized she was staring at my crotch. Finally she just reached out and grabbed my dick, saying "Can I have some?"

"No, you cannot!" knocking her hand aside. "Just keep you hands to yourself."

She smiled, "Good idea." She leaned back against

the back of the tub. Her hands went to breasts, then to her nipples, then one hand slid down her body and between her legs. She started rubbing her pussy and moving around and moaning.

"Shit," I said, and stood up and grabbed my towel and stomped out of the building. I looked down and realized I may have been disgusted, but my dick wasn't. I had quite a boner. A couple of the sunbathing chicks giggled and stared. I wrapped my towel around me and waded back across the river and got dressed.

I had breakfast with my friends. They had decided to spend the rest of the day at the Springs, so I said my goodbyes, fired up the bike and headed back over the steep little hill leading up out of the Verde River. I went back to Camp Verde and spent a couple of hours touring Montezuma's castle, an old Indian cliff dwelling there. Then I headed south toward Phoenix.

The high country Arizona air soon changed to something short of a steel town blast furnace as I dropped off the hill down toward Black Canyon City. Up high on the right the lofty peak of Crown King looked down almost like it was saying, "Man, I wouldn't go down there!" I hit the bottom of the hill and hung a left over toward Carefree and Cave Creek, then turned south on Cave Creek Road. The Harley was thirsty, so I hit the Shell station at Cave Creek and Bell Road. I pulled up next to a guy fueling an old Honda converted dirt bike. It had been stripped, the rear shocks welded in top position, big knobby tires, big rear sprocket, and straight pipes.

I asked him "Hey, how does it go?"

He turned, "Goes OK. Not real well balanced, little too heavy in the nose. I would like to able to buy one of those factory made dirt bikes one of these days."

I grinned, "Yeah, a little pricy for an afternoon toy." He nodded yes.

We finished gassing up. He said he was going across the street and get a couple of tacos, and since I hadn't had anything since breakfast, I decided to join him.

As we munched our tacos and washed them down with Pepsi Cola, we fell into a conversation. I had mentioned that I had done a couple of tours in 'Nam. He looked a bit perplexed.

"Yeah, I was in Vietnam in 1962. I admire you for doing two tours, not sure I could have done that!"

"Yeah, what do you do now?"

He answered "I drive a truck. A fuel truck. We haul oil and gas and diesel around the state."

I nodded. "Do you like it?"

He smiled, "I do. It is the first thing in years that I have done that I do like. Back to this Vietnam thing. When I first got back, I was so pissed off at the world. I had about twenty jobs in the first two and a half years. I just couldn't get used to someone standing over my shoulder, telling me what to do. Military told me just to go home and forget about everything and just assimilate, but they didn't tell me how."

I was quite taken aback with his declaration. It explained exactly how I felt, but I was kinda shocked to hear it come out of someone else's mouth.

I slid off the stool and said "Man, that is exactly how I feel. And I have had about the same kinda luck with jobs. Maybe I should think about driving when I get through with my little trip. Hey, give me your ticket, lunch is on me. My name is Evan Smith."

"Well, thanks Evan. I'm Larry Murley. You know, the thing I like about trucking is, you are the one making the decisions. I like the solitude, and I just love seeing new country. One of these days, I hope to get a long haul job."

We climbed on our bikes, reached over and shook hands, and parted ways. I felt like I had met a kindred spirit.

I drove south to where the road became Sunny Slope Boulevard. I idled down the curvy little roads lined with VW micro buses, tie-died sheets and bearded characters loitering about. Past the little art shops, to where it became 7th Street - or Avenue, I can't remember which. It was getting late in the afternoon when I found the bike shop that had been recommended to me. I asked the guy if they had time to service the Harley and tighten all the things that had loosened up. He said no problem.

As the sun was setting I rolled up Grand Avenue and headed out towards Wickenburg. The irrigated orchards and fields along side of the highway made the late afternoon air pleasant. Off to the north stood the mountains and Crown King that I had driven alongside that afternoon. I found a restaurant in Wickenburg and had dinner, then drove west to where the hills dropped off into flat desert. I pulled the Harley off to the side of the road far enough away to distance myself from the traffic, not that there was that much. I sat down on a flat rock and leaned back and closed my eyes. Just for a second.

Two hours later, a Coyote yip about thirty yards away brought me wide awake. I pulled back on the highway and cranked it on. The lights of the little town of Aguila winked at me in the distance. I idled down slightly until I cleared the little curve on the west side of town, then turned up the throttle again. I was sitting on about 70, the road lay flat out before me.

A set of headlights were getting steadily brighter and closer in my mirrors. Finally they swung out around and a shiny black Kenworth roared by me. As he passed, I could see about six inches of flames standing above the stacks at times. He slowly pulled on away from me and by the time I reached the next little town he was gone, outta sight. Maybe there was something to this truck driving world I thought. I made a mental note to check it out.

Coming down out of the mountains, rolling toward San Diego, the air was soft and warm on my face after the hot blast of the De Anza desert. I rolled through the little town of El Cajon, and down El Cajon Boulevard. There were lots of cool bikes parked along the curbs, lots of denim vests with colors sewn on the backs. Tough looking guys, long hair and beards, with hard looks toward me. Think I will just keep riding.

Downtown San Diego there were sailors everywhere. Lots of lights. I turned south on old 101, then Imperial Beach. I looked for the rows of cottages about a block off the beach. There, that's the number. I swung into the parking spot next to the 57 Chevy Apache truck, let the engine idle a second, then cut it off. The door opened to the little duplex, a head looked around the door. Then the door swung wide, and a cute blonde with bare tits jumped off the couch and headed for a bedroom door.

"Evan Smith! You sorry piece of shit! I'm sorry, Sergeant Evan Smith! You sorry piece of shit! Come into my house. Shelly, get your cute little ass out here and say hello to the best damned soldier that ever humped the 'Nam!"

The girl appeared from out of the other room, wearing a sleeveless shirt that served to enhance the perfect little tits.

"Hello Evan" she purred, "I have heard so much about you."

"Hope you didn't believe everything this asshole told you, Shelly. Good to meet you!"

She took my hand. I almost felt like I was getting a hand job on my right forefinger as she smiled at me. I turned and Rich and I bear hugged each other.

"When did you get out Evan? God, it's good to see you. I wasn't sure I ever would. Things got awfully hot over there after I left. I kept track as much as I could."

"Couple'o three months ago. Been working odd

jobs, not having much luck holding a job. So I bought a bike and decided I would take a vacation, so here I am."

We talked till the wee ours of the morning. Shelly had gotten tired and gone to bed. Finally, Rich said he had to work tomorrow, then he would be off for the weekend and we could do something. It sounded good to me, I was tired too.

I slept like a rock. I dreamed of far away places, I was lying in a warm pool and the water was washing over me. Then I realized I wasn't alone. A naked Shelly was sliding her sweet lips up and down my hard cock, but I realized it too late. I erupted with everything I had into her warm mouth, yelling at the top of my lungs, "SHELLY!" My brain came back into focus. I sat up on the couch where I had been sleeping. She looked at me and smiled the sweetest, happiest, smile that you could ever see. She wiped her lips and said, "Thanks, I needed that."

I scolded her, "*You* needed that? Rich is my buddy, my friend. I would never do something like that with a friend's girl." She went on to explain that she and Rich were friends, but this was the 60's, and

42

she was not going to limit herself to just one guy, and Rich had other friends as well.

"Besides, you were lying there, with the biggest old boner you could imagine. I just couldn't resist it."

"Well, let's just try a little harder while I'm here. I'm not really into that kinda thing."

She pouted, "What's the matter, wasn't I good?"

"I don't remember anything 'cept the end."

"Well, come on. I'll do some more, so you can see how good I am," she said as she reached for me.

"*SHELLY!* Go put some clothes on, and I will take you to breakfast. Not that you are hungry."

She giggled and swished her cute little ass to the other room, looking back over her shoulder and saying something about how she was always hungry. Oh God, why does this shit have to happen to me? She reappeared moments later in a pair of red jean cutoffs - that were really cutoff – and a sleeveless shirt unbuttoned and tied at the bottom under her tits. Wow.

I fired the Harley and let it warm up for a few minutes, then backed around so I would have a straight shot out to the street, then nodded for Shelly to jump on behind me. She stepped on the left peg, and through her leg over and scooted her self right up against me. She leaned back and we were gone down the street. She leaned those cute tits up against my back and said to hang a right at the next intersection. I did so. As I throttled up the street she pointed out a building on the left. I pulled in and stopped just to the left of the door. She hopped off and shook her hair out. It looked perfect anyway. We found a booth and the waitress took our order.

I spent another few days with Rich and Shelly, and somehow managed to keep her off me. Something in my upbringing just made that type of action uncomfortable.

We played tourist, and visited all kind of places. One of the outstanding things was an evening visit to Tijuana. We took Rich's truck. He said it probably wasn't a good idea to take the Harley across the border.

We walked the streets with lines of shops and bars. Everything was for sale, and I do mean everything. Shelly said she had always wanted to see one of the sex shows. I didn't. I couldn't help being reminded of some of the similarity of Tijuana and some of the towns in 'Nam. It wasn't too bad until dark, then I started getting the same feelings I had while in 'Nam, as if there was an ambush somewhere just ahead. As we turned down this one side street, some Mexican guy steps in front of us and says "Señors, Señorita, come see our show. It is very nasty, you will like it."

I reached out to brush him aside and pass, but Shelly yelled, "Oh come on! Let's go! It'll be fun!"

I didn't think so, but Rich said, "We'll try it. But when I say we leave, we leave!"

"OK," she answered.

We went inside. The room was dimly lit except for a light over a platform in the middle of the room. It was raised about a foot off the floor. A Mexican girl was selling beer. She was topless. She could have been attractive, but seemed to be

45

burned out, lifeless. I wasn't surprised. I didn't like this place. All my senses were right on edge.

In a couple of minutes two more attractive women stepped from the shadows and onto the small stage. Music began to play, and the girls started caressing and kissing each other in some type of suggestive dance. Shelly was all smiles, she liked this. She looked at me and said slyly, "I like girls too," and turned back to watch the show. I wasn't surprised at this bit of information. I had never thought much about girls having sex with other girls at this point, but there were probably a lot of things I was naive about. Including what was fixing to happen on stage.

The girls had just about covered all of each others bodies with fingers and lips and tongues, when out came two more girls leading a small donkey, a jack. They led him to the stage and a small low table was brought in and one of the girls lay back on the table. You can probably guess what happened next.

I said, "Shit, I don't need to see this!"

Rich said "Okay, me neither!"

We grabbed Shelly between us and headed for the door. As we got there, the Mexican dude with one of his buddies was blocking the way.

"Señor, you have not paid yet! That will be $200 for you and your friends."

I never stopped. I took out the dude and Rich got his buddy, and we hit the street in a dead run, heading for the more populated better lighted district. We never stopped until we found a crowd and got lost in it. We made our way back to the truck and said goodbye to Old Mexico.

It was sometime the next day I strapped my gear on the bike, said goodbye to my friends and headed up the coast. I stopped at San Juan Capistrano and spent a half day, digesting the history of the old mission. I was impressed with the history of the country that I had grown up in, much of which I knew little of.

I, like many of my brothers in arms, thought we were fighting for our country in Vietnam. We were told it was to stop the spread of communism. This wasn't true. Although for a while we did some good, assisting the people of South Vietnam. But with politics and protestors, that pretty much turned to shit by the time I left. Poor people, I felt sorry for them. We just left them high and dry.

I rolled on up the coast, stopping here and there, where ever and when ever something caught my eye.

I stopped for lunch one day in a little town called Coalinga. A local burger joint caught my eye, so I wheeled the bike into a parking place under a shady tree. I went in and bought a burger and fries and a cold Dr. Pepper.

I sat on a bench and ate while taking in the local landscape of rolling hills. It was quite pleasing to the eye.

Suddenly, the earth beneath my feet shifted! I damned near fell off the table I was sitting on. The Harley lay over on it side, then the ground shook again, and again. I scrambled to my feet, the burger and fries tightly grasped in each hand. The Dr. Pepper lay under the table, as if he was playing 'duck and cover'. Then it was quiet again. I looked around. No one else seemed to be paying any attention. I finished up my burger and fries. I set the

Harley up again. No damage, except a little dust, which I promptly wiped off. I went inside and got me a glass of water to wash down the rest of the food.

"Say, anything get broken in the quake a few minutes ago?"

The girl looked at me, "That was no quake, it was just a little tremor."

Okay.....

I toured San Jose, The Bay Area, Oakland, and checked out the Haight-Asbury District. It just looked like a rundown area of town, with a bunch of rundown people. So I just rolled through. I headed out of town to take a look at the Redwoods and the Bristlecone Pines and Sutter's Mill, and all the historic spots I had read about. Sometimes staying in campgrounds, sometimes I got a motel room. I met lots of people, some on vacation with their kids. The guys would eye my bike, and ask me where I had been, tell me they envy me. I would look at their families, and tell them they have nothing to envy me for. They should be proud of what they have.

I was amazed at the mixed reactions of people when I would tell them, I had returned a short time ago from Vietnam. Some would clasp my hand and say they were happy to see me home and unharmed and out of that terrible place. Others would look at me and suddenly find somewhere else to be, as if I had leprosy or something else they could catch. But it always seemed when I met another vet, there was a brotherhood there, regardless of what war they had served in, or when.

I spent some time at the top of Donner Pass, thinking of what it would take to make a person want to eat another. I couldn't come up with an answer.

I looked east towards Reno and the Nevada wastelands. I decided I wasn't done with the west coast, so I turned the bike back downhill toward Sacramento and through it until I hit I-5 again. Then on up the coast. California is so different, so varied. I found the farther north I went, the more I liked it. Up through Redland, it was getting damn nice, then I crossed the line into Oregon. Shortly after, I saw a sign for a big rest area. I took the exit, the sun has dropped beneath the mountains to the west. As I circled under the Interstate, the roar of a river rose above the pulsing of the Harley. I found a spot and parked. I got off and shook off the vibration numbness. I went down and sat by the river. Now this was peace. I didn't want to move. The mountains, the air, the water. It was all mesmerizing.

I sat until well after dark, until I realized hunger was starting to gnaw at me. I always kept some crackers and sardines in my saddle-bags for times like these. I was just setting down at the table provided for weary travelers, about to open my sardines, when a soft southern drawl said, "Aww, come on now, don't eat those. My friends and I have a fire going over here. Come join us."

I looked around to see a rather tall girl dressed rather cowboy-ish jeans, cowboy boots, black t-shirt, and straw hat with a decorated band, and silver and turquoise jewelry.

She said, "Hi, I'm Cat."

"Hi, I'm Evan."

She told me to follow her, and I did. she had a

long stride, but I managed to keep up. We arrived at 3 or so eighteen wheelers backed into parking places. They had a fire going in one of the built in Bar-B-Que pits the rest area provided. There was chicken and steaks sizzling on the grill, and a table was nearby filed with containers of potato salad, beans, chips, and various condiments.

Cat started the conversation.

"Hey, everybody! This is Evan. He is a hungry biker. Thought we might feed him before he eats sardines by his self."

There were echoes of "Hey, Evan!" "Welcome, wanna beer?" "Find a seat, foods about done!"

I did as I was told. Soon I was sharing a delicious meal with a bunch of people I had never seen in my life, but I couldn't have felt more at home than if I was with family.

After dinner was over, they all took turns more or less in introducing themselves, and getting acquainted. They seemed sincerely interested in finding out all about me, and they were the most interesting lot I had found since my buddies in

Vietnam. Indeed, one of them was a vet from '66 and '67, a Marine.

We sat for hours. They only slightly knew each other, but had been running together for a day or so when one of them had mentioned this place. And since they or their loads had time, they decided to stop here. And with luck, so did I.

I sat and listened that evening as they talked trucking, about the freedom they had, the places they had been, loads they had hauled. It seemed like such a good life. The more of these people I came across, the more intrigued I became with their life. I asked lots of questions; about the trucks, about their lives. I wanted to know more.

Cat asked, "Evan, have you ever been inside a big truck?"

I shook my head no.

"Well, come here then."

There were laughs and shouts of "Cat, if'fen you are in there more than 5 minutes, we are gonna call for a preacher!"

She turned and yelled "Now y'all just shut yer faces. I promise, I'll be gentle!"

I follow her up into the Peterbilt long nose. She let me sit in the driver's seat. I took the big steering wheel in my hand. It felt natural, as if, in some former life, I might have set here before. I looked for the shifter, and found two. She saw the confusion in my eyes.

"This is a 5 and a 3 transmission. It has 5 speeds in the main box with an auxiliary of 3 gears. That gives you 15 gears. The truck has a 335 Cummins engine. I wouldn't recommend this transmission to a beginner though, more like a RT 10 or 15. Much easier to learn."

She showed me the brakes and other gauges and lights and their uses.

Then she smiled. "Follow me to the bedroom." She slid out of the passenger seat back through a curtain into a room with a half size bed, decorated in Indian blankets and dream catchers and feathers. Several pictures were on the walls. One of them was her with an older man. She saw me looking at it.

"Evan, this was my dad. He died a year ago. This was his truck. He taught me all about driving, and the business. Now it's my life."

"Wow, Cat, I am impressed. You are pretty amazing, I would have had no idea. I am getting interested in trucks. When I get through with this little ride, maybe I will give it a try."

She smiled, and squeezed my knee. "We better get back outside before they start thinking dirty thoughts!"

"Let's go, wouldn't have that!"

We rejoined the others as a joint was being passed around. I took a hit off it, and sat back and thought of my new friends. Shortly, some one said, "Well, if I'm gonna deliver in Portland anytime tomorrow, I need to get some sleep." The thought was echoed by most of the others. We all shook hands, and I thanked them for their hospitality. I agreed to keep my eyes open for them in the future.

When I got around to Cat, I reached out my hand for hers, but instead she wrapped her arms around me and hugged me really tight, then kissed me quickly on the lips, saying, "Evan, you see the sign on my door? Look me up, I would love to see you again. Oh, yeah, if you get up to Portland in the next few days, come over to the Jubitz. It's a big truck stop. The first street south of the I-5 bridge going over to Washington. We always seem to get held up there for a few days waitin' on loads."

The next morning before daylight I heard the three big diesels come to life, and few minutes, they eased out of the park and up the ramp. I could still hear the gear changes as they climbed up out of the river valley, then I drifted back into dreams of white lines and wide vistas of beautiful scenery.

In the next day or so I visited Klamath Falls, Crater Lake, and dozens more beautiful spots in the Oregon wilderness. Truly, one of the most beautiful places I had ever been, and the friendliest. I slept under the stars, and thought of my future. I decided no more jobs. That demanded I stay in one place, oft times under a supervisor who didn't deserve his position. Out here I was the most relaxed I had ever been, since before I had joined the Army and had gone to the 'Nam. I liked that feeling.

About three days later, I came out of the wilderness and turned on I-5 again. The sign said *Portland 25 miles*. I looked around at the farms. Good grief, it looked like this place could feed the world. My thoughts went to Cat's last words. Hmmm, what was that place called? The *Jubitz*? Just south of the Columbia River Bridge she had said.

I steered the Bike through late afternoon traffic, down through the maze of elevated overpasses, till I saw a sign. Jubitz Truck Stop, exit 307. I steered my way off the ramp and turned right. Down the road a ways I saw the sign. A minute later, I pulled into a parking place. I shut the bike off, and proceeded to pack away my jacket and chaps and helmet. I looked at the long lines of trucks parked in neat rows to the front and side of the building. Nothing looked familiar.

I went inside, found the restroom and washed off a bunch of road grime and made myself a bit more presentable. Then I turned toward the restaurant, and slid into a seat in a booth along the wall by a window. I had a good view of the parking lot.

The waitress came and I ordered a steak and

mashed potatoes and green beans and a glass of ice tea. As she turned away with my order, someone slid into the booth with me. It was Cat!

"Hey, you made it!"

I turned and hugged her. "I sure did. Wasn't sure you would still be here, but here I am!"

"That's great. Yeah, I have a load out going to Shakey, day after tomorrow."

"Shakey?"

"Yeah, truck driver talk for L.A."

"So, you have all the cities named?"

She laughed, "No, not all of them. Just some of the bigger ones."

"Tell me more, what are some of them?"

"Oh, we call New York, or Jersey, *The Dirty Side* or *The Dirty*. Let's see, Montgomery, Alabama is *Smoke City*. Houston is *The Astrodome*. Texas in general we call *The Lone Star*. St. Louis is *The Gateway*, Fort

58

Worth, is *Cow Town.* Arizona is *The Cactus Patch.* You get the idea."

"Yeah, I get the idea."

I found myself really liking this woman. She was genuine, no games, no pretense. She was who she was.

My food came and we continued to talk all through the meal. It seemed as if we had to know everything about each other immediately.

After eating, we went out to the big service center for the trucks. She was getting an oil change and lube on her truck. I marveled at the big trucks with their cabs jacked or hoods pulled over to expose their motors. All the mechanics were busy, but seem to enjoy their work. They finished her truck. She paid the bill, turned to me and said, "Jump in!" I did as I was told.

She pulled the truck through the bay and out the door and around the building. She pulled in front of a refrigerated trailer, then slowly backed into it. I felt the touch of the truck to the trailer, then she eased out on the clutch a bit more and the fifth wheel slid under the trailer, and bang! We stopped.

She slipped the tranny into a forward gear and tugged on the trailer, the hitch was locked. She set the brake and opened her door and stepped out, I did the same from the passenger side. I walked around, she climbed up on the platform between truck and trailer and hooked up the air lines and plugged in the trailer lights. She turned to me and said "By the way, when you back up to the trailer, you should always get out and hook up the air lines and apply the brakes before you back under, so there is no chance the trailer will roll, but it had only been a short while so I didn't."

I grinned. "You could have run that right by me, I would have never known."

Cat smiled, "I didn't know if you knew or not, I just didn't want you to think I was careless about anything."

"Cat, I would never take you for a careless person about anything."

Another smile. "Good, cause I'm not!"

We went back to the truck stop. As we approached the building, Cat told me she had a room in the hotel there and that I was welcome to come up and shower, so I should grab me some clothes. I thanked her, and grabbed my bags off the bike. We went upstairs. It was a small room but clean and comfortable. She told me to make myself comfortable, she had to check on some things and would be back in a few minutes.

When she left, I got undressed, turned on the water and luxuriated for probably too long, but it felt good. Life on a bike, although enjoyable, tends to get one on the funky side sometimes. I dried off and wrapped my towel around me and stepped in front of the mirror. I had let my beard grow for the past couple of months, I was looking a bit like a wild man. I shaved my neck and trimmed my beard and mustache, shaped my hair a bit, and stepped back to assess my work. At 25, I was still physically fit from military life and hard physical work. I had no bad habits, other than I would smoke a little weed once I a while, but only when my day was over, and would drink a beer with my friends. But I had about a two beer limit. I looked at my upper body looking back at me. I had a couple of battle scars, nothing serious. A bullet from an AK-47 had grazed my left shoulder, and a fragment from a mortar had cut my ribcage on my right side just below my breast, neither had needed more than field dressing. I had been lucky.

I had not heard the door open and close, until the low wolf whistle brought me back to reality. I turned to see Cat smiling.

"Oh, thanks! Been a long time since I had anyone whistle at me."

She laughed, "Well, you deserve it. You are a fine specimen, Evan. Now get your self dressed, and meet me downstairs. It's time for me to have my reconditioning time."

I closed the bathroom door and pulled on clean underwear and new jeans and a nice western shirt I had bought in Arizona. I came out, slipped into my boots, and stood and saluted, saying "Ma'am, the place is yours."

I went downstairs and watched a couple of drivers trying to compete telling the biggest lie. I decided it was a tie. About that time I heard someone tuning up a guitar behind a curtain. I stuck my nose through and to my satisfaction I saw a honky-tonk of grand portions; two bandstands and two dance floors. This is just too much fun, I thought.

About then I heard a couple of whistles behind me. I turned and just about lost it.

It was Cat. She was dressed in a little black dress with spaghetti straps. Her hair was down, falling across her shoulders. She was wearing heels and hose. Her make up was flawless, not much, but just enough to accent her face and eyes. Oh. My. God. She was a knock-out. I might have been able to say something to her or perhaps dress the two drivers down for whistling, but my mind turned to mush and my jaw dropped to my chest. Finally, my voice came back.

"My God, Cat, you are beautiful! I always thought you were pretty, but you are beautiful."

"Thanks, Evan, it's nice of you. Sometimes I forget about being a girl, driving a truck all the time. Now, let's go have a slight snack, before we go have fun."

We returned to the restaurant, and had a light

dinner. I have no idea what I ate, it could have been mud, I was so entranced with the woman before me.

After dinner, we went back to the club. The band that night did some western and some rock-a-billy. We danced a few times, had a beer or two. Cat had friends, occasionally someone would ask her to dance, and she would be away, then she would be back. I was having the time of my life. When the band picked a slow love song, we stepped to the dance floor. Cat put her arms around me and lay her head on my shoulder, we danced a slow dance, with our bodies touching each other, I wanted the moment to go on forever, I didn't want this feeling to go away. And I guess it made me a bit nervous. About midnight, she looked up and said "Let's get some air."

We walked outside the door of the truck stop. It was a warm evening in late summer, a soft rain was falling. We stood there together, under the canopy.

"Evan, I have had the best time tonight. Thank you so much. You are such fun to be with, and such a good dancer, too."

"It has been my pleasure, Cat. It has been a long time since I have enjoyed anything so much. Not since I went to Asia."

"Well, I was going to suggest a walk, but looks like the rain gods don't want that. Let's go upstairs and talk some more."

I followed Cat back to her room. It was so easy to talk to her, I found myself running my mouth like a teenage boy. Something that wasn't at all like me. She unlocked the door, we entered. She closed the door behind us and turned to face me, and immediately her arms went around my neck. Her lips met mine in a dizzying, mind-blurring feeling of contact. We found ourselves crossways on the bed, kissing, holding our bodies tightly together, as if we felt there was some force in the universe that might be set on tearing us apart. Seconds ran into minutes that felt timeless. Our clothes had slowly left our bodies, because they would not allow every square inch of our skin to touch. That was the most important thing in the world to us. Hours past, and slowly the room came back into focus. Our hearts slowed together, till they beat at a normal rhythm. Still, our bodies refused to move apart. We lay facing each other, our hands clasped together at our breasts, gazing into each others eyes, and tracing the wonder of the others face. Cat was the first to speak.

"Evan, I don't know what just happened, but it wasn't in the planning. My life is pretty well set, as what I must do and not do. But I just couldn't help myself. I wanted to know everything about you, and I guess this was a part of it."

"I understand that, Cat. I am not ready for something like this to happen to me, but I am glad it did. I so respect what you do and who you are. We will work it out."

We lay and talked - for a few minutes, we thought - until the morning light started to filter through the window. We noticed it at about the same moment. We both smiled and cuddled closer together, and drifted into sleep, still with hands clasped together.

We awoke about 10 o'clock. Almost together, we said, "I'm hungry!" and then laughed. After another hug and a couple of sweet, light, caressing kisses, we got slowly out of bed. She went to the bathroom first, then I heard the shower running, I asked if I would be welcome, and got a yes. I quickly used the bathroom and slipped into the shower behind her. I gasped as I looked at her nude body for the first time. She was lean and trim, but not lacking any of the essential girl parts that attract a guy. She had curves where she needed them. I took the soap and wash cloth and proceeded to wash the beautiful back, all the way down to the backside. She turned to face me. Oh, my! Her breasts were firm, not large but beautifully shaped, and set high. I washed them as well. Cat came close and kissed my neck and shoulders, then my chest and stomach. At that point I told her to stop, or we would be found dead in the motel room of starvation. She giggled and stepped out, leaving me alone to finish washing away the evidence from the night before.

We made our way down to the restaurant and stuffed ourselves with enough breakfast to kill a couple of field hands, giggling like school kids and playing footsie's under the table.

After we finished we went outside. It was a beautiful day. I turned to Cat.

"Would you like to go for a motorcycle ride?"

"Oh Yeah, if I can be the navigator! I know some

cool spots."

"Let's get you a helmet, and grab jackets."

A few minutes later, we hung a left on I-5 onto I-84, also known as Columbia River Highway. Up about exit 28 Cat directed me off the road and into a park.

We parked the bike and walked to the base of the most incredible waterfall I had ever seen. Bridal Veil Falls is spectacular. We walked and soaked up some of nature's most beautiful work. We rode another few miles and found another falls, and then another. We spent the entire day riding and looking at this massive river. We visited the memorial where Lewis and Clark had first viewed this country, and we talked. Boy, did we talk. There was so much to know about the other, and so little time. Soon, it was time to turn the bike west again. We rode down the canyon as the setting sun lit up the hills to our north, while for the most part, we rode through the shadows and curves. We stopped again at the Jubitz, just after dark. We had stopped at a local eatery on our way back, so we went straight to our room, showered and changed. We went back to the Lounge, and sipped a beer and listened to the band.

We danced a couple of slow dances. Cat looked up and said "Let's go to the room!"

"Okay by me," I whispered back.

We made love, but mostly we just lay for hours talking. It would have to last us for a while. We didn't have any idea when we would be able to see each other again. Her contracts were mostly up and down the west coast, and occasionally Arizona and Nevada. I was slowly working my way east as the year was winding down. This trip by no means was ever meant to last more than the summer, and the sun was already starting its journey back to the south.

Soon, we drifted off to dreamland, wrapped securely in each others arms. In what seemed to be only a short time, her alarm went off.

We turned to face each other. "Evan, as bad as I don't want to, I must be a big girl about this. I have so enjoyed every second of our time together. But I have a loading appointment in an hour and a half. You can stay here, no need of you getting up this early, but I must go."

I took her face between my hands, and kissed her softly on the lips. "Cat, do your thing. But I will not lay here in bed. I am going to watch you till that cute little back end of your truck disappears from sight. We have each others contacts. We are going to be together again, count on it."

We dressed and collected our gear, and I followed her out to her truck, leaving my bags by the bike. She unlocked the Pete and started the engine for a warm-up. She tossed her bags in the jump seat. She turned and threw her arms around my neck, and gave me a heart-jumping kiss.

"Evan, I am not going to shed tears. So I'm escaping before I do. I am outta here!"

She hopped up in the cab, rolled her window down, slipped the tranny into a gear, cleared her brakes, and turned, with just a hint of a tear in her eyes, blew me a kiss, and was gone.

I stood and watched her leave the parking lot and turn right, and slowly disappear from my sight. I walked back to my bike, suddenly feeling lonely for the first time in a very long time.

A grizzled old truck driver, dressed in jeans, a denim vest, and a black western hat, looked at me and said, "The Jubitz worked it's magic again, huh?"

I looked at him. "Yeah, driver, I guess it did it's part."

I threw my leg over the Harley, kicked it to life, and rode out up the road. I turned right onto I-5 and crossed the Columbia into Washington State. I had passed the truck Port of Entry several miles up the road before the smell of Cat and the warmth of her touch had faded from my mind. Was this Love?

I hung around the Olympia, Seattle area for a few days, but I just couldn't seem to find an interest there. Finally, one morning, I loaded up and headed east, out past the huge aircraft factories, and toward the mountains, up through Snowquallame Pass, and out across the broad expanses. About 5 hours later, I roll into Spokane, found a motel, and settled in for the night. I turned on the TV and watched the evening news. Still more Vietnam footage. I strained my eyes, searching for a familiar face, but got no reward for my efforts. *It needs to end, those poor people.* For years their lives have never seen peace.

I awoke next morning, my head was cluttered with thoughts of my future, with Cat, with the scenes of Vietnam from last night's news. I felt confused, depressed. I just wanted to escape all these feelings. I headed east, up and over into Idaho, thru Coeur d' Alene and down into Montana. Songs ran thru my head. *"I gotta get out of this place." "Running through the jungle."* Strange thoughts.

I cranked the throttle on. I raced through Missoula, then, just as I was coming into Butte, I looked in my mirror at the red lights that had appeared out of nowhere. Shit, I thought. I pulled to the side. I killed the engine, kicked the kickstand in place, and just sat there.

The Highway Patrolman walked up and looked at me. "Sir, up here in Montana, we are not really finicky about our speed limit. But sometimes we just hav'ta stop people and remind them if they kill themselves, it's just a whole lot of extra paperwork."

I looked at him. A slight built, red-haired man, his name tag said Manus.

"Officer Manus, I am sorry. I don't usually do stuff like that. I am just having a bad day today. I think something in my past is catching up, and I guess I was just trying to get away."

"Sir, may I ask, were you in Vietnam?"

"Yes Sir. Two tours."

"Mr. ...... uh"?

"Smith, Sir."

"Mr. Smith, would you follow me down here to Butte? There is a small truck stop on the right. I'll buy you a cup of coffee."

"Sure, lead out."

He went back to his car and I followed. On reaching the truck stop, I followed the HP officer in. We found a booth. He ordered a cup of coffee, I ordered iced tea.

"Mr. Smith...."

"Evan."

"Evan. I wanted to talk to you a few minutes. Not as a police official, but just as another guy who has been to Southeast Asia."

"You were in 'Nam?"

"Yeah, back early in the spring of '62. We went over to teach the ARVN how to run and set up radar. My duty was pretty easy. The most difficult was getting shot at on our way up to Monkey Mountain, up above Da Nang. But strange things happened back then. One of our guys, he was a couple of years older than the rest of us, arrived with us. But the day after we arrived, he was pulled out of our group. I never saw him again after that. One of the guys I knew said he saw him with another guy, over at Pleiku once. Said they were dressed in civvies. Then, later on that spring, another one of our group said they saw him in a jeep, and he looked like he was all fucked up. He was ragged and dirty, and all cut up, said they took him to the hospital in Da Nang. They said he didn't answer to his name, claimed his name was "Boots." I don't remember what his last name was, his first name was Larry. But, I just told you that to let you know how bad that place screwed up some men's lives. After I came home I went into police work, and in the course of that time, I have run into a lot of boys that went to Vietnam and came home wrecks. I have started trying to talk some to maybe see if I can help some. My father was in Germany during WWII, and he was a mess the rest of his life. He was a good man, but he was haunted his whole life."

Could I ask where you are headed?"

"No where in particular," I answered, "just riding. Taking the summer to sort my life out."

"I would like to suggest that you go out here east a ways out of Butte, before you get to Bozeman, and turn South down to Yellowstone and go camping for a week or two. Just get away from society, and live with nature. It is one of the most beautiful places in the country. Lots of the boys that have returned from 'Nam have told me that it is one of the few places they find any peace. Just go and set there, and contemplate the majesty that is there, and compare it to what man does. Maybe it will help some. But don't try to run from your ghosts. You might run into something worse."

"That is not a bad idea, that going camping thing. I think I will take you up on that."

We talked for about an hour, about Vietnam, and life and law enforcement, and then he said he must get back on patrol. We said our goodbyes and I watched him leave the truck stop. Maybe it was just the feeling that another person cared, or maybe someone I could talk to about those bad times over there. But whatever the reason, I felt better. I fired up the Harley and went into downtown Butte and went shopping for camping stuff. Nothing fancy, just a few things that would make things a bit more comfortable for a few days in the woods. I had dinner at a mom and pops cafe, then found a cheap motel. It was starting to drizzle, so I rolled the bike into the room and put a piece of cardboard box under it in case it leaked. I decided no TV tonight, so I spent the evening writing a letter to Cat. That wasn't an easy chore, so many things, that I found difficult to say on paper. But I manage to tell her all the news, and that I was going camping for a while. I awoke next morning, and, as an after thought, I stopped at a hock shop downtown. I went inside and looked at the handguns; I picked out a .45 revolver. It wasn't pretty or new, but I figured I might need something in case a hungry mountain cat came calling. I was about to pay for it, when I spied a used 35 mm camera in the case. I asked the guy how much. He told me, he also said it had been his camera. He reached back and got a new one on the counter, and said he had just picked it up, and decided to sell the old one. He gave me a good deal on the pistol and the camera and a couple or three rolls of film. I packed them into the saddle bags, stopped by a food store and picked up some canned foods and pasta, and few other things, and headed for the great outdoors.

It was late afternoon by the time I got over the mountain and had drooped down into the park. The cop had been right, it was beautiful. I camped in a campground as it was late. I had a bite to eat and was soon asleep.

It was late September. I found it difficult to believe it had been only three months since I had pulled out on I-30 just west of Hope, Arkansas. Now, the summer was fading into fall, and not far behind would come winter. Winter in the northwest would not be a friendly place for a homeless biker.

I decided that while I was here I would enjoy this spot of creation that so may visited every year. Peak tourism time was over, most camp sites were empty. Some days I would hike aimlessly, marveling in the beauty around me. I took dozens of photos, the 3 rolls of film, didn't last long, but I was able to find places to buy more. I was in awe of the buffalo and the elk. It was rutting season for the elk, and I would spend sleepless hours, listening to the bugling. Sometimes a bull would call, then another in a different direction, then another, and another. I wondered if they were challenging each other, or if they were trying to call the cows to them. I confess I was a bit ignorant of their habits. I saw bear, both brown and black, and thought one morning that I heard a wolf howl on a distant ridge. I asked a Ranger about it later that day. He said it was possible. It was believed that all the wolves had been killed out, but maybe one or two could still be around. He said that there had been talk of returning the wolves to the park, to help control the elk herds that were having a negative impact on the park. I walked through the geyser area quite a lot, and watched Old Faithful spring to life, always right on time. I was curious about all these things, and as I pondered them, I found that Officer Manus was right. It did kinda put humanity into a different perspective. All these functions of nature, carried on daily, and had been doing so for thousands of years, without help from man. Meanwhile, the childish futile actions of man seemed to be getting him nowhere, except closer to extinction.

I spent a day or so and climbed out to the top of the rim of the Caldera, and stood and looked at the expanse of the ancient volcano. It was miles around it. After about two weeks of this nature retreat, the wanderlust got the best of me. I broke my last camp, and loaded up my bike. I cruised up to the gate of the park, and told the Ranger so long. He had been a wealth of information since I had been there. He pointed me in the direction of Jackson Hole, my next stop.

When I arrived in Jackson Hole, my heart almost stopped at the sight of the Grand Tetons. Their immenseness was.....grand! I visited all the tourist spots, then decided one morning when I awoke to find my bike covered in a heavy frost, it might be time to go farther south. So south I went, down across Wyoming. The farther south I went, the less appealing the state became. I hit I-80 at Rock Springs late in the evening and found a cheap motel.

I had not heard from Cat all this time. So, I called

the number for her office. The dispatcher answered. I identified my self and told him I was looking for Cat or would like to leave a message for her. He told me to hold on and put me on hold. A minute later the phone clicked.

"Evan Smith, where are you? I have missed you so much!"

"Hi, Cat. I am in a little town called Rock Springs, Wyoming, and God I have missed you, too!"

We talked for about an hour. I told her about my travels, about Yellowstone. She told me about her trips. I told her I had a bunch of pictures to send her once I had them developed. Finally, after making more connection plans, we said our goodbyes.

The next morning I headed east toward Laramie. Couple of hours later, I stopped for fuel in Rawlins. I saw a sign about a hot springs in a town called Saratoga. A few miles farther east, a sign appeared with an arrow pointing south, saying *Saratoga*. I backed the throttle off a few notches, then decided I would do it. I turned south, heading for the mountains. Less than an hour later I pulled into the Hot Springs parking lot. I spent the afternoon lolling about in the warm water, soaking out longtime soreness and stiffness from sleeping on the ground, and the numbness that comes from long hours on a Harley Davidson. I had sent my pictures about a week before to Fojo to have them developed, and had asked them to be returned to a General Delivery box in Laramie. I was anxious to see them but was afraid they hadn't made it yet. So I decided to spend the night in Saratoga. I walked around downtown late in the evening. People were friendly, and would stop a stranger on the street for a conversation. It seemed that some of the chaos going on in the rest of the world never seemed to touch this little town tucked in the foothills of the Medicine Bow National Forest. I found a cheap room and spent the night. Next morning the temptation was too great and I returned to the hot pool again for a couple of hours. Then I headed up the mountain. I was told that it was a much prettier ride and I would still wind up in Laramie. It was a beautiful ride. I stopped on top at Libby Flats, it still had little patches of ice from the previous winter's snow. I looked all around and back to the South at the Colorado Rockies. My thoughts were still how beautiful the country was. I idled the next few miles off the mountain, down through Historic Old Centennial, Wyoming, and drove on to Laramie.

I found the Post Office in Laramie, and, after showing some ID, I picked up my pictures. I fueled the bike, but by then it was starting to get late, and the weather seemed to have a bite to it. I picked up old US 287, and headed south.

I shivered as I climbed out of the flats towards Colorado. It had gotten cloudy, and now the temperature was dropping. I had donned my leathers and heavy jacket at the truck stop. Now, with the mountains to the west of me blocking what little sun was coming through, I cranked the Harley on. The road was straight to the Colorado line. At the top of the hill, the *Welcome to Colorado* sign appeared out of the darkening roadside. I wound my way through the curves. Virginia Dale, the old stage stop, flashed by on my left. I rode fast in the cold evening, thinking about a warm motel room in Fort Collins a few miles down the road. The Forks, a restaurant and store in the little burg of Livermore, went by on the right. I leaned to the left and climbed up the side of the hogback, then through the gap and down. No lights were headed at me on the straight away ahead of me so I turned the throttle up a little bit more. A big boulder the size of a haystack lit up in my headlight on the right side of the highway, then a curve sign appeared signaling a right hand curve. I throttled back a bit. At just that moment, something went over my head, right in front of my handle bars. A deer! I cut my speed quickly. Just then, another, on my right. I leaned left, barely missing the young doe, then another. I swerved right, missed again, there, two more. I went between them. I was just about to congratulate myself when the big buck landed about four feet in front of my front wheel. I didn't miss him. The impact was hard, the Harley went airborne, and that's no small thing for a Harley. I went up over the handlebars, and as it came down it rolled to the left side, leaving me sliding along down US 287 behind the big bike, sparks lighting up the night. It felt like time had stopped. I rolled over and slid on the other side for a few moments. The pavement felt hot, I felt hot. The chill from a few minutes ago was gone. Finally, I stopped. I lay on my back for a minute. Hmmm, the stars were all out in Colorado. I was pretty sure they were stars. I moved my legs, then my arms, then started checking myself out. Being an ex-combat vet, I knew better than take anything for granted. I had seen guys loose a leg in combat and get up and try to run off. But everything seemed intact. Next I will try to stand up, I thought. Yep, I can stand. Everything seemed intact. By the time I had gotten up, an eighteen wheeler had pulled up close behind me. I heard his air brakes set, and saw his four way flashers come on. Next thing I hear, "Hey, Hand! You ok? You better sit down here for a minute, get yourself checked out. That was a hell of a crash, I could see fire flying a half mile back!"

I answered, "Yeah, I'm ok. I need to check my bike."

I walked another thirty or forty feet up the road. The Harley was laying on the right shoulder. It was a mess. Forks bent, handlebars all messed up, oil everywhere, dents and dings and just a damned mess. My heart sank. What now? That was pretty much my life. I was standing there looking down at my most prized possession, when a voice behind me asked, "Are you the rider?"

I turned to face a Colorado Highway Patrolman. I hadn't even seen the red and blue lights come up.

"Yes Sir."

"What happened?" he asked.

"A whole herd of deer, or at least seven or eight that I saw. I missed three or four barely. The last one, a big buck, landed right in front of me."

The trucker chimed in. "Yes Sir, he's right back there behind my truck, in the middle of the road, deader than dead!"

The trooper asked, "You need to go to the hospital?"

"No Sir, I'm ok. I am gonna need someone to move my bike though."

Before the trooper can say anything the trucker said, "Hey, I have an empty lowboy back there. Let's get some help and throw it on it and we'll figure out what to do with it later. We need to get you out of the weather and a cup a coffee in you. If that's ok with you, Officer?"

The trooper nodded his approval, adding for me to go by the Larimer County Sherriff's department in the morning and fill out an accident report. I agreed to that. The trucker - Frenchy, his named turned out to be - brought his rig up along side my bike. With the help of some cowboys that had stopped we rolled the bike up and Frenchy quickly strapped it down. I climbed up in the big truck, a Kenworth, and sat down in the air ride jump seat. My eyes went to the dash with all its gauges and lights and switches. Something inside me said this looks like home.

We drove about two or three miles farther and pulled into a cafe called Vern's. We got out and went inside. The walls were lined with mounted trophy deer and elk and all other kinds of game. I wasn't quite ready to look at more deer right at that moment. We found a booth, and as I was about to sit, I noticed everyone in the room was staring at me. I looked at Frenchy. He read my thoughts.

"Maybe you better go in the bathroom and rearrange yourself."

For the first time since the crash, I looked at myself. My leathers were burned off me, and were in bad shape. My jacket had huge holes in the shoulders and elbows, and I had blood on my hands, and face. Wow. I took off my leather chaps, one leg of my jeans was torn pretty good. My hands had small scrapes and the side of my face had a bit of road rash, but I was really lucky. I removed my jacket, and carried it and my chaps out and dumped them, in the back of the booth. The cute little waitress looks at me as she pours the coffee and remarks, "You clean up real good, after wresslin' Bambi like that!"

Frenchy had told my story while I was cleaning up. I nodded. "Thanks, Hon, but you can't see the inside." She smiled and walked away.

After dinner we drove from La Porte on down to Fort Collins. Frenchy found a motel on the north side of town that he could pull his rig into. We went a got a room with two beds. We sat and talked for hours. When I told Frenchy that I had been to Vietnam, he let up.

"Mon ami! I fought the Viet Minh in 1958 and 1959. I was at Hue when it fell."

The comparison of the two wars filled our conversation. He told me that there were Americans involved in that war as well, something that I didn't know. They weren't fighting as infantry, they were probably CIA, but they were there. He told me that he went back to France, but came to America soon after coming home. He had worked in New Jersey for a moving company for a while, then a chance acquaintance got him into heavy equipment. He learned to drive a truck, then got into hauling heavy equipment. He got a green card, then in a few years was able to become a citizen. His family in France helped him finance a truck and trailer. Now, here he was, an independent businessman. An American dream come true. My friend Andre Dupree was going to turn out to be an angel - a guardian angel - come to earth. After talking late, we arose next morning and walked across the street to a small cafe and had breakfast. I was moving quite slowly. I was sore and stiff, but I had been lucky.

We found out from a guy in the cafe that there was a bike shop down the street just before the Old Town Area of Fort Collins. We drove down and found a place in front the rig could be squeezed into. The owner of the shop came out and took a look at the Harley.

"Is that deer fur I see on that fork?"

"Yes sir."

"You come out of this pretty good. Yeah, the bike can be fixed. Gonna take a while though. Not gonna be cheap either. I can give you an estimate later today, after I make some calls."

"Okay, fix it up."

Frenchy turned to me. "Ami, have you given any thought as to what you are going to do now?"

"No Sir. I suppose I am going to get a job doing something. This looks like a nice little town, maybe I will try here."

"Evan, would you consider working for me? I am on my way to Fort Carson; I have a contract to move some military equipment to other military post around the country. Some of it will be physical, and I will need some help. I will teach you to drive, and help you get your commercial license. Whaddya say?"

My head spun. What a chance to try out something I had been thinking about for a month or so!

"Hell, YES, Andre! You won't be sorry. I just thank you for giving me the opportunity. I have been thinking about this for a couple of months, but didn't know where to start!"

"It's settled then, partner," and stuck out his hand for me to shake. I grabbed it and answered.

"Partner!"

We hadn't even notices the CSP cruiser that pulled up, until the voice said, "You okay this morning?"

I turned and said "Yessir! I am more than okay!"

"Have you been over and filled out an accident report?"

"No Sir, that's next on the list this morning!"

"Look, if you like, since your wheels are sorta in a pile, I will drive you over. It won't take but a few minutes. Probably have you back by the time they get the bike unloaded."

I nodded yes, and Frenchy did too. As the officer drove me over, I told him about Frenchy's offer.

He said he thought that was a good deal, and

wished me the best. I filled out the report and he dropped me off and waved goodbye. I took a card from the bike shop and promised to call them later in the day to find out the damages, and approve the repair. I climbed up in the Kenworth, and French fired it up and we were off. I had no idea what to expect, or where the next stop was, but who cares, I felt good about this.

We took Colorado 14 out of Fort Collins to Interstate 25. Just after we cleared the port, Frenchy pulled into a rest area about a mile down the Interstate. He parked the rig, and stepped out. I was watching to see what he was going to do when he said, "Slide over in the driver's seat!"

Oh Shit! This was happening must faster than I thought. I figured a few days of loading and unloading, maybe a big parking lot or something. But no, here and now.

He climbed in the jump seat, and sat down.

"So now comes the first lesson. We have about 50 miles of highway in front of us. Nothing to do but drive, maybe pass, but pretty simple. First of all, I have a 1693 series Caterpillar engine in here. You will have to take a little time to get used to how the RPM's rise and fall, that is the key to a smooth shift. You will do a double clutch at first, later on we will learn other methods. Since we are empty you will start off in second gear. Look up on the front there, see the pattern on that little plaque? That is the order you shift into. When you start off, push your clutch all the way to the floor, that enables the clutch brake to stop the tranny from turning. Then you put it in gear. Next, you don't give it any throttle until your clutch is out and you are moving. Then bring your RPMS up to 2100. Then, while holding the throttle at that level, you let off ever so slightly, while pushing in on your clutch and moving your shifter into neutral, then clutching again you let your RPMS fall to 1800 thereabouts and slip your shifter into the next gear. And you simply go through the pattern, until you have it in the highest gear you want to be in for the speed limit, or that the engine can maintain the RPMS in a pull. Do it. It's yours. And, oh yeah, you will make mistakes."

I took a deep breathe, and pushed the clutch to the floor. I put my hand on the shifter and pulled it into the second gear position. I let out slowly on the clutch, the big truck rolled forward, I gave it a little fuel, and it picked up speed. But I noticed I was at

2100 almost immediately. I had watched Frenchy, so I did as he had said. It was a little rough, but I was in the next gear, and then the next, 'till I maxed at fifth gear. I came out of the fourth hole and flipped my switch and came across the box to the sixth position, and it went in, with a little lurch by now. I was out of the rest area, and on the approach to the highway. I took a look in the big mirror on my left. The lane was clear. I changed back into the hole for seventh which was where I had started originally with second. Through each gear the time between shifts grew longer, giving me more time to think about it. Finally, I was in tenth gear, and rolling at about 65. I heaved a sigh, and settled back into the seat. I looked over at Frenchy. He was beaming.

"Sacre bleu, Evan! That was well done! Better than any first timer I have ever seen. My friend, I believe you are a natural."

"Thanks, man. I was a bit nervous, especially at the fifth to sixth move."

"Yes, all you need is practice now. Shifting under a heavy load needs to be bit more precise and sometimes faster, or you will lose RPMS and sometimes lose a gear and have to drop down, but you will figure that out when the time comes. Ok, enjoy the ride for a while. We will switch back before Denver, until you get more practice."

So went my first time behind the wheel of a big rig. In the days and weeks ahead, I would gain more and more experience. Frenchy was a good teacher.

He never put me into a dangerous spot, or one past my ability to handle. I learned to drive on curves and in mountains where shifting was a constant thing. I learned to pull heavy loads, and to judge my stopping distances. I learned to tie down loads safely and how to watch all six sides of my truck and its load. I learned how to drive off steep mountain grades, and keep my brakes from overheating. By the time winter hit, I was doing well. Frenchy was based out of Texas, but ran all the western states, and now with his contract was even venturing east sometimes. About two months after he had picked me up we went to his home near Austin, Texas. He took me down to the motor vehicle office, and I picked up a drivers manual. I studied it some and went and took my Class A commercial test and passed it. He then took me to a clinic and I took a physical for a DOT health card. I passed it, too.

We went out that night and celebrated. I was now a fully certified truck driver, and I couldn't have been happier.

Now I was more valuable to Frenchy. I could drive thru the ports of entry now, and I had a log book, which meant as long as we weren't hauling oversize loads we could team it and cover twice the miles.

Occasionally, if he needed time off, I would make a trip by myself. Life was good.

Oh, Yeah, I was still talking and writing letters to Cat. It had been three or more months since I had seen her. So when Frenchy told me we had a load of military equipment going to the Port of Long Beach for over seas shipment, the first thing I did was call her dispatcher and tell him I was coming to California. By now he considered himself our dating service. He said he would make sure she was in town.

About five days later my rig was empty at Long Beach Port. I called her office and Dan the dispatcher answered. He told me to drive over to their yard and, Oh, by the way, she was there. But he had not told her I was coming; this was to be a surprise. I did as I was directed and an hour later turned into their yard. I parked the truck and headed for the office. I walked in and through a narrow hallway I could see a cute behind in a nice pair of jeans leaning over the high counter with her back to me.

As I approached, I heard her say, "Dan, are you pissed at me about something?"

"No, why?"

"Cause I haven't gotten a decent load in a week or more, that's why!"

About that time I took the opportunity to say, "Oh, I wonder if I could get a job application?"

Cat half turned and looked at me, then turned away, then back as she realized who I was.

"Evan Smith, you sorry son of a bitch!" Then she saw Danny laughing his ass off.

"Danny, you sorry fucker! Both of you should be shot, as soon as I am through with you, Evan!" And at that, both arms went around my neck and the sweetest lips were trying to devour my mouth. Cries of *"get a room"* echoed from the other drivers in the room.

When I was finally able to breathe again, I said, "Well, I guess you are glad to see me, huh?"

"Oh, I am glad to see you, mixed with wanting to kill you! Do have any idea how hard that is on someone's heart? C'mon, let's get out of here, and out of the range of these leering bastards. Danny, can he leave his rig here in the yard?"

Danny nodded yes and told one of the yard men to find a place to put it out of the way. I went outside and parked and got my bag out of the side box, climbed in Cat's car and away we went.

We spent the rest of the afternoon catching up on several things. First our bodies, then my new trucking career. I showed her the pictures of my trip to Yellowstone, and the bike after its mishap with Bambi. All this without loosing touch of a single square inch of her delicious body. We talked until after dark, then arose and went out and had dinner, then back to bed. We slept until 10 in the morning. We were two lost souls clinging to each other, knowing full well their time was limited, but still reassured that it wouldn't be as long as the last time. I had chosen a career matching hers, with that freedom that allows you the whole country of America as your backyard. It was just being able to navigate that back yard to our satisfaction was the key. We would master that in the coming months.

We were able to glean two days and two nights before my load back to Texas came up. She watched me drive away, as did I her the first time we parted. Again, I noticed it took miles and hours before the sweet perfume of her body left my nose and my senses. And I could feel the touch of her skin for days. I tried to shake it out of my mind, but I think I knew then, I was falling in love.

1970 came to an end. I was sitting in the 76 truck stop at Eloy on New Years Eve. As I sat and listened to the countdown on my truck radio, I wondered what this year would bring. 1970 had been a huge turning point in my life, how much more could happen?

When the clock hit midnight, all the truck horns went off. Fireworks erupted from across the road. People were firing rockets and shooting firecrackers. For a moment, I went all tight inside. Memories of other fireworks of a less festive nature popped into my mind, and I got this cold feeling, of anger, and fear. Then it was gone, and I came back to the present. People who shoot fireworks for fun probably have no idea what effect they have on a combat vet, or maybe they just don't care.

About that time, there was a knock on my truck door. I rolled the window down. There in the darkness was a young girl. She looked up.

"Can I get in your truck? I am cold!"

"Sure, go around. The door is not locked."

She opened the passenger door and climbed in. She was dressed in a fairly short skirt, and a long jacket. Her hair was quite disheveled. She was quite made up for one who looked so young.

"Would you like some company?"

"Not particularly. Just don't want you freezing, it is a chilly night!"

"You mean you would say no to this?" She opened her coat to reveal a pretty set of bare breasts. Her skirt was already up, and it was plain to see, she wore no underwear.

"Hey! Cover yourself back up, don't do that! Who are you? Better yet, how old are you?"

She pulled her coat back partially. "I'm 18. My name is Angie."

"What year were you born?"

She hesitated. "Yeah, that's what I thought," I said. I wasn't particularly surprised at the young girl being a prostitute. Many of the working girls in Vietnam had been very young, in many cases just children.

"Angie, you gotta get out of here. I am not going to pay you for anything. I would never do that."

"Mister, do you see that guy over there? If I get

out with no money, he is going to be mad and he is going to hit me."

I looked at the man she was pointing out. He was standing in the shadows of the building.

I said," Angie, get out of the truck."

As she exited the truck, I stepped out of the truck and walked to the man in the shadows.

"Hey, man. If you touch that little girl, I am going to have your ass. I am not into prostitutes, and I am not going to give her money, especially now that I know your sorry ass is going to get it. So just do the both of us a favor, and get the fuck outta here!"

I barely saw the knife come out of the coat until it was slicing through air at me. I caught the blade in my jacket sleeve, just above the wrist. Its blade cut deep, and I felt the burn. I hit the guy once in the solar plexus, hard, straight in, in kind of an uppercut. I stepped back, bringing my foot up and catching the guy full in the face with my boot, straightening him up. I then pulled a good roundhouse kick to the side of the guys head. He went down like a bag of sand.

I looked at the blood running down my hand. By then I was coming back to reality a bit. God, I hope I didn't kill him!

By then, there were about a dozen truck drivers gathered about. One of them looked at me and said "Man, that was beautiful!"

The sheriff deputies arrived about then. They asked me what had happened. I told them my side of the story. A couple of bystanders backed me up on it. One of the deputies went around the building and came back leading the young girl, Angie.

He asked "Angie, is this true, what this man said?"

Angie nodded the affirmative. By then I had my jacket off. The knife had done a good job, but had hit nothing vital, like a tendon or artery.

One of the deputies said, "Let me run you over to Casa Grande and get a couple of stitches." I nodded ok, and walked back to my truck and locked it up.

They had loaded Mr. Pimp into an ambulance,

and was hauling him away. Angie was being put into another deputy's car. I stepped into the first patrol car, and started the short ride to the hospital.

The deputy turned and said, "Bud, you are very lucky. That guy's a bad guy. You probably don't know but Angie is his daughter. He is has been pimping her for about two years that we know of. She is still barely 16. We have been after him for a while, now he is gonna go away for a long time."

I thought for a minute. "The sorry bastard" was all I could say.

About three in the morning I was delivered back to the truck stop. I decided maybe just have an early breakfast and get on my way.

I walked into the restaurant, and everyone there stood up and cheered and applauded.

I just kinda smiled and waved.

I ordered breakfast, and the waitress came with it quicker than I expected. She set my plate down and slid into the seat opposite me.

"My friend, you are a bit of a hero here, you know. We all knew about Angie, but couldn't seem to help. No one could ever seem to catch him at it. You brought a bad thing to an end. Angie's mother died several years ago, but her grandparents are still living, and that is where she is headed. The cops have got her old man on everything from pimping to assault with a deadly weapon to a dozen other things. He is going to jail, and he will never be allowed to touch that child again. She told us that if we saw you, to thank you, and she apologizes for her behavior toward you. Breakfast is on the house, and will be for a long time, and we want to see you back here every chance you get. We like your kind of people."

I looked at her, "I don't know what to say but thank you!"

As I finished eating, people would come by and pat me on the shoulder, or women would take me by the hand and say thank you.

I finished my meal and left, still a bit confused by the events of the morning.

1971 went by like power line poles on a dark

desert highway; discernible, but not worth the conversation. I was able to meet Cat every few weeks and spend time with her. Her company opened a terminal in Tucson, Arizona, which gave her more opportunities to come my way. Frenchy had a lot of heavy haul going that way. So much so that another miracle happened. In December, my Christmas present was a brand new Powder Blue Kenworth Hood, extra long hood actually, to fit the 1693 series Caterpillar engine into. I had a stretched sleeper for extra comfort. OTR trucking was just starting to evolve and big sleepers were becoming more commonplace. Sometimes we needed to spend time waiting for loads, and it was less expensive to live in our sleepers than in motels. I bought the new truck with a five speed main and a four speed auxiliary tranny to move those big loads in rough terrain. It had polished aluminum fuel tanks, shiny wheels and twin stacks. It was beautiful. Frenchy helped me buy it, since he had hired another driver to drive his older truck.

He bought a couple of other trailers as well. The mines in Arizona were doing well, and it seemed the country was in a growth spurt. When heavy haul would slow down, I would grab the reefer trailer and haul a load of frozen foods or garbage for someone. That way I kept busy. Cat's dispatcher helped me out with that as well, pulling some loads for him.

So maybe '71 was worth discussing after all.

I spent a lot of time in truck stops showering, eating, and sleeping. Gradually they became centers for socialization as well. I met a lot of drivers, and we would occasionally find ourselves in the same truck stops at the same time. I found a great many of them were returning soldiers and marines from Vietnam. Men who found it difficult to fit back into their communities, but found a new freedom piloting their big trucks all around America. Men who were used to thinking for themselves, and just weren't comfortable being shut away in a cubicle or a factory.

The truck stops were starting to evolve a bit as well. Many were beginning to have stores in them, carrying the necessities for traveling folk. Many had good food in their cafes as well. By the early 1970's there was just beginning to be a touch of the dark side to some of them, not as much as there would be later.

Sometime in late '72, Frenchy told me he wanted to take me to dinner. I made it back to our yard that afternoon. He was quiet as we finished the business of the day and drove to a local steakhouse. We talked business through dinner. We talked about maybe adding another truck to the company. We were still doing a lot of work for the mines out in Arizona.

Finally, with dinner finished, Frenchy took a drink of tea, then wiped his mouth with a napkin.

"Evan, I have something to tell you. This isn't easy for me, but bare with me. I have been going to the doctor over the last couple of months. He gave me some bad news. I am not going to live much longer and I am going to get much weaker over the next few months. There is nothing they can do. I have a tumor on my brain. they can't reach it, it's pretty final."

I sat for a minute or two, stricken speechless as it was.

"Frenchy, I don't even know what to say, except I am so very sorry! Whatever you need from me is yours, for as long as it takes. I mean that. You have evidently known this for a while. Do you have plans? What do you need from me?"

"Evan, I want you to buy the Company from me, I want you to have it. It isn't much of a sale, as it is a bequeath. I don't want money, just stay with me and give me a home and a life till it's over. We will transfer the paperwork immediately. I want it taken care of before something happens."

"Whatever you want, my friend, we will do it."

Life had just gotten serious again. I was losing probably the best friend I had ever had. He had given me a leg up out of the foxhole and had given me cover till I was secure now on my own. And all I could do was wait and watch. I asked if there was family still in France or anywhere else. He said no, his parents had passed not long ago. When he had become an American he had picked a spot out west of Austin in the Hill Country he had bought himself a burial plot and had arranged the whole thing.

In the next days we sat and talked about our lives. I felt that now I really wanted to know everything I could about him. It is strange that you can have a friend, and be content with the most casual knowledge of him or her, but when that time left with that person is threatened, it becomes suddenly important to know all about them. I had spent time with men in combat that I never knew much more than their name, and maybe where they were from. But they could become seriously wounded or worse, and then they became like a brother. It is strange how the mind works.

Frenchy was cognizant for the most part the rest of October and November, he seemed sometimes to slip away and become distant for short periods. But I never saw him frown, I never heard him complain. I asked him if he wanted a service. He said no, no preacher or anything. He said I knew who his friends were. I could let them know, and if we wanted to send him off with a few kind words, he would like that. And, oh yeah, tell all the truckers out there that knew him that Ol' Frenchy would see them on the flip-flop! I had to smile at that. He said he didn't fear death, he had made his peace with that years ago in Indochina.

Just a week or more before Christmas I had a load over in L.A. coming this way, so I brokered me a cheap load over to pay for the trip. Frenchy said he wanted to go. I jumped at the chance. I called Cat and told her we were coming over. I had already explained Frenchy's condition to her. She said she would be there. We arrived on December 23, dumped my load and went and loaded my back load. Then we drove over to Cat's terminal. We went in and I started introducing Frenchy to all the drivers, and handshakes were going around. We were led back to the back room where a bunch of the driver's wives and families waited. There was a big table filled with food.

Danny said, "Hey, Evan, when we found out you were coming over, we decided to have our company party a day or so early. Kinda give you and Cat a big Christmas present! And we are happy to welcome Mr. Frenchy here to share Christmas with us!"

I looked at Cat. She shook her head no, she hadn't told them about Frenchy.

The evening was grand. Laughter, tall stories about the "Old Days" of truck driving, good food. Some of the kids sang Christmas carols. Danny told Cat and I to get out of the building we were ruining the evening for everyone else with our smoldering looks. He said he would find Frenchy a place for the evening. Evidently Frenchy was having a good time with his new friends.

The next day Frenchy asked if there was a beach nearby. I looked at Cat. She said yes, it was not far. So we loaded up and Cat drove us down to Malibu Beach. It was a sunny warm day for Christmas Eve, and as we walked along, Frenchy took off his shoes and socks, and walked barefoot in the sand, sometimes wading into the low surf.

"Evan, when I was a young boy my parents would take me to the South of France to the beautiful beaches there. I love the ocean and the sun and the sand, the sound of people laughing and enjoying themselves. I just wanted to feel that one more time. It is a good day. Thank you and Cat for giving me this."

Cat ran to him, tears streaming down her face, putting her arms around him and hugging him.

"Now, now, Miss Cat, none of that crying stuff. I will take all the hugs I can get from such a pretty mam'selle, but no tears!"

"I'm sorry Frenchy, it just isn't fair! Forgive me."

She wiped her eyes but continued to walk with her arms around him. We had a great Christmas with our California friends, but on the 26th we left fairly early, waving goodbye as we drove out the gate. The next five days I was busy with end of year stuff.

On New Years Eve, about 10 in the evening, Frenchy called me to his room. I noticed he seemed to have a rather crooked expression on his face.

"Evan, thank you so much. You have made the last couple of years of my life the best. It was fate that had me following you down that dark Colorado highway that evening. But now it is time to go, I feel it. Stay here with me a while."

I sat with him and talked. About a quarter to midnight, Frenchy pulled out onto that unknown highway that has no map, nor white lines, because it's a one way road. R.I.P. mon ami, Au Revoir!

I never suspected that he had so many friends. I probably should have, he was a good guy. But being a truck driver you spend so much time in the solitude of your truck, I thought, maybe, well, I was wrong. The word went out, and people started dropping by our yard. I had his remains brought to our terminal for viewing late on the afternoon before the burial the next day.

People dropped their trailers in other locations, and bob tailed to come see Frenchy for the last time. Soon they were filling our yard and parking up and down the road on both sides. Thankfully, Cat flew in that afternoon. I don't know what I would have done without her.

I guess you don't have to be Irish to have a wake, 'cause man, we had a wake! The evening was spent with food and toasts to Frenchy; everyone had his or her favorite Frenchy story. I listened to as many as I could. It seemed many had the same thread; Frenchy helping someone out when they most needed it. There were some funny ones though. My favorite, I think, was a story a driver told about him and Frenchy up in Colorado on an icy road once. It seems they were taking a load up over Loveland Pass, and it was a cold snowy morning. They had started up the east bound side and were some distance behind a snow plow, but were obviously catching up. He said Frenchy was just jumping up and down yelling, "Alle! Alle!" and bunch of other words he didn't understand. But just after they made the last switchback before the top, they caught the plow. When Frenchy tried to shift down his tires broke traction and he stalled.

Frenchy put the parking brake on which locked the truck tires, but when he took his foot off the brake, the truck started to slide backwards! He quickly applied the brake again and it stopped. So Frenchy pulled the Johnson bar or the separate trailer brake down, and when he took his foot off the brake the truck stayed. Frenchy had looked at his co-driver and said "Ok, we gotta chain up now," and he opened the door and stepped out, and promptly disappeared. The co-driver opened his door and looked down and Frenchy was lying on the other side of the truck, his feet had slipped out and he had slid completely under the truck! That is how slick it was!

It took both of them some time to hang two sets of doubles on the tractor and get them secured, but when Frenchy tried to move the big rig forward, it just spun. So he had to back down the mountain road to the switchback, where the road leveled somewhat, and get a start. Once they did they made the top. On the down hill side in second gear, the steering tires would slide out on some of the switchbacks. Just one of those days a trucker must deal with.

Many of the drivers came and told me that Frenchy had got them jobs and got them started in the trucking world, and they weren't a bit too big and tough to shed a tear or wipe an eye, or blow their nose in to a handkerchief as they walked by his casket. The mortuary had dressed Frenchy in a black suit and tie. I couldn't help thinking it wasn't appropriate, I had never seen him look like that. But he looked good. One driver expressed it best, with "Damn, ol' Frenchy looks like he could'a been a college professor or sumthin'!" Yeah, he could'a been. But he loved driving trucks, and all of us understood that. Next day, I called the Sheriff's office, and told him that the funeral procession was going to be quite long and filled with big trucks. The deputy said yeah, he had expected that when he heard the news. He said Frenchy was one of the good guys, and was sad to hear he had passed.

About 11 am the hearse arrived, and Frenchy was loaded up and away we went. As we traveled through the Texas countryside, we would meet other trucks and cars. We had procession of over a hundred trucks, and people would not only pull over when we went by, but most would get out and remove their hats. Yeah, I guess he had friends. At the graveside we just all kinda said farewell in our own ways, and tossed some memento into the grave as we passed or spilled a bit of earth. I didn't stay long, I had said my goodbyes. I knew for sure Frenchy wouldn't want any sad hangers on, so Cat and I went back to our yard. It seemed so empty and abandoned. Frenchy's Kenworth sat next to the fence, just inside the gate, like a faithful friend waiting for his master to come home. Sorry big truck, not this time.

I had relied on Frenchy from the time we had first met for his business knowledge and experience, now the responsibility was all mine. I had watched our slow times and our busy times. I decided that the company should diversify somewhat.

I went and bought two refrigerated 45 foot trailers. When loads got light in heavy haul, we could do a little garbage, or frozen stuff, heck even maybe a little meat. I knew this would take me east, but I decided it was a must to stay solvent. I hired my first team, and put them on Frenchy's old truck.

They were a couple, nice people, both in their mid to late 30's. They looked a bit cowboy-ish in their jeans and boots, with feathers clipped to their hats.

We negotiated pay and arrived at a figure we were both agreeable with and a few days later, Jim and Jo were headed for The Valley to pick a load of produce headed for Philadelphia. After about a month or so, I realized one day I was not going to just sit on my butt in the office, I was going back on the road. It was about that time that Tony came into the office.

Now, Tony wasn't much to look at, nor was he a great conversationalist. But Tony was a truck broker. He could find loads when there wasn't any loads. And I don't mean junk freight either. Good, paying loads. He had contacts all over the U.S. Tony wanted a chunk of the company though, he had worked a lot of years for firms that didn't appreciate him, and had walked away from jobs that left him nothing. He was willing to work for less wages if he could get a percentage. And he came with Michelle, as a package deal. Michelle was a Virgo, and Miss Organization Herself. I had our lawyer come in and we set up a contract with Tony and Michelle. They would run the business end, I would have final say on disputed matters, and I could get back in my truck and just drive. Hooray!

1973 came and went. Our company was growing fast. We had added one more truck and one more team. Everyone stayed very busy. We also had two owner-operators that leased to us if we got too over whelmed. It was early '74 one evening when I had just gotten in off a run. I had no sooner stepped out of my truck when Jim and Jo pulled into the yard. I walked over to say hello. I stepped up on the running board on the passenger side of the truck and looked through the rolled down window and had two beautiful boobies staring at me! Creamy, tanned boobies with dark brown hard little nipples. I quickly stepped back off the running board. Jo stuck her head out the window and yelled, "Hey! Didn't you like 'em?"

My answer was, "They are very nice. But do you ride around like that a lot?"

By then I had climbed back onto the running board. Jo had pulled on a shirt.

"Not all the time, but I do a lot. Keeps Jim's spirits up on those nights of long, lonesome highways."

Jim looked across. "Keeps a lot of other drivers awake, too! Well, just the other night we were out there on that long road in Nebraska. There was this driver in front of us, weaving back and forth. First on the shoulder, then across the line. I grabbed my mike on my CB - I noticed he had antennas on his truck. I hollered, 'Hey, Jones Transport! You got your ears on?' I was about to do it again, when he came back, 'Yeah, you got the Jones.' I answered back, 'Driver, you ok? You're wobblin' a lot!' He came back, 'Yeah, I'm kinda worn out, but I got about another two hours and a half to get this load where it needs to be. Gotta make it somehow.' I looked at Jo. She grinned and started shuckin' her clothes. That always gets me excited, too. I waited a minute or so, until there wasn't any traffic behind me. Then I said 'Driver, drop down to channel 13.' He said 'Ok.' I said 'Now, you hold on to your steering wheel, and watch out your window." I pulled out and eased up beside him, and as I got along side, I switched on my cab lights.

"You never saw a driver straighten up as fast in your life! Jo turned to face him and put him on a little show! She put her hands under those sweet little tits and kinda lifted them up, and slid her hand out along them rolling her nipples between her

120

fingers. Then she stood up and put one foot in the seat and showed him her pretty little pussy. She played with it for a few minutes then blew him a kiss and settled back in her seat and put her feet up on the dash. I turned off the lights and mashed my motor, and we went on down the road.

"I called back, 'Driver, you gonna be okay now?' He came back with, 'Fuckin A! You couldn't put me to sleep now with a hammer! I will remember that for the rest of my life. And you may have just saved it, I was gettin' to tired to drive. Thank YOU and thank you little lady! You are beautiful!"

I had to ask, "Don't you ever get jealous, sharing your girl with other guys like that?"

"No, Evan. We have been together about 15 years now. It keeps excitement in our lives. I know she is going to wake up beside me every morning. She doesn't go off with other guys and party. What we do about stuff like that we do together. Besides, after that that night I got one of the best blow-jobs you could ever imagine!"

Jo nodded affirmative, and replied, "But none of the other drivers that work here will ever know. We keep it among our friends and strangers."

"By the way, Jim," I asked, "I have been seeing a lot of these CB radios showing up in trucks. Are they worth having?"

"Yes Sir! They sure are. First of all, they are company on long hauls. They help get directions, road conditions, weather reports, Smokey reports. Just generally helpful in a whole lot of ways."

"Hmmm. Would you mind helping me get one installed and show me something about it?"

"Sure thing, let's get this thing unhooked and parked. I know a good radio shop near here."

Couple of hours later found us at a CB shop out near the truck stop.

Jim showed me around, telling me about some of the better radios, what kinds of antennas worked best, the pros and cons of linears. I wasn't totally sold on the idea, although I did see some advantages. Radios were the life blood of the combat vet. I would have hated to have been without one for an extended period.

I settled on a Cobra 29, and a set of twin antennas. I did listen to Jim's advise and bought a noise canceling microphone for it, but declined the linear. I paid the happy shop keeper, and we loaded up our wares and headed back for our yard. Upon arrival, we pulled my truck into the shop and turned on all the lights. Jim went into the wiring harness, found a live terminal that was apart from lights and ignition, and ran a fused wire off it. He then located a ground, and run a wire off it. We hung the radio in the center of the ceiling up front near the overhead console. Then he ran the wires up and hooked them into the radio's harness. Soon the antennas were mounted on the top bar of the outside mirrors, and the coaxial cable routed through into the cab, hidden in the trim, along with power cables.

An external speaker was added, and the noise canceling the mic replaced the original mic. Jim went and got his SWR meter and set the standing waves, and my new toy was ready to talk. Jim explained that in most cases, channel 19 was the recognized trucker channel, with the example of some places in California, and on a couple of other highways, where they used 21. The other channels were mostly used for private conversation.

As we worked, Jim started telling about things he had heard over the radio. Once, he said, he was following a guy off a snowy pass up in Colorado. They had been talking; the driver in front of him was hauling an empty fuel tanker. He said all at once the guy just quit talking. Jim said he kept asking, "Hey, where did you go?" But the guy didn't answer. Finally, the guy came back on the radio.

He said, "Sorry about that. All of a sudden I looked back and my trailer was trying to pass me. I got it back straight and then it went the other way, then back the other way. For a while there I thought I was going to lose it and I dropped my mic, and it took a while to get myself together and get back with you."

Jim said it was about that time he came upon the guy's trailer tracks and sure enough for almost a quarter mile, the tracks went from one side to the other. He told me many other stories. I became fascinated with stories that came off the road.

Jim said, "OK, boss, what is going to be your new handle, your CB code name?"

I thought about it. Back in Vietnam we had this Cobra pilot. He was one cool dude. He saved our asses so many times. His call sign was Wind Walker. I thought about it. I couldn't do no better. I looked at Jim.

"Call me Wind Walker."

"Wind Walker." He nodded yes.

Jo said, "Boss, that is really a good one." She handed me the mic, "Here, break it in."

I laughed and pushed her hand aside, "No, hun, I am too shy for that. I'm gonna ease my way into this. You warm it up for me."

Jo slid up into the drivers seat, adjusted the volume and the squelch level, held the mic up to her pouty little lips and said, "Break 19."

Suddenly the previously quiet radio burst into a jumble of squealing and noise. Jo grinned and squealed.

A strong radio signal overpowered the rest, and a strong voice, said, "Hello darling, who we got there?"

Jo answered, "They call me Nitro."

"Nitro, huh? Why do they call you that?"

"'Cause nitro comes in small packages, and I am really small. Everywhere."

I confess, I blushed at her frankness.

The man came back, "Well, sweetheart, what's your 20? Maybe we should get together, and just see how small you really are!" There was a low, deep laugh with that.

"Well, driver, that really sounds like fun. But I will catch you on the flip flop, cause I got two big old guys here to take care of me tonight. See ya! I'ma gone gone!" She purred. She reached up and turned the radio off before the driver could answer. She said, "Well, that should warm it up," and we all laughed.

I looked at Jim. He was laughing his ass off. I felt plumb vanilla beside these two!

I thanked him for helping, and offered to pay for his work. He declined saying it was his pleasure, that he enjoyed doing it.

Next morning, we - meaning me running solo and Jim and Jo running team - headed for The Valley down by Harlingen for a load of produce headed to Philly. We got loaded late that afternoon, and started for the dirty side. I was running two log books, and still having trouble keeping up with the team. I wanted another driver. I had talked to several, but no one clicked. I had talked to Cat several times, but she was not going to ever leave her job and her truck and her friends and family in California. The last few times we had been together we had argued about it. It was affecting our relationship.

It wasn't just that, either. I hated the long absences from her and since I had started to spend so much time on the road, the meetings got to be less and less. I found myself looking at other women more and more. Sometimes I would meet old friends that ran as couples and they would have cookouts or parties on long layovers. I had been propositioned many times. It was just the way people were on the road, they seemed to take their pleasures where they found them.

I got my load off about 30 hours later. Our broker had a load of furniture going to Florida, but we had about 24 hours before it loaded. Jim and Jo were in the same situation. It was snowing. We were hanging in a 76 truck stop on I-95, just south of Hartford.

There was a rap on my passenger window, I looked and it was Jim. I motioned him up, and he swung up into the jumps seat.

"Boss, my dad is driving down to get me to come home for the evening. I would like Jo to stay here with you if she could. She and my folks don't hit it off. I will be back tomorrow evening, if that's alright. Mom hasn't been well, and I thought I would take the opportunity."

"Sure, Jim. She can hang with me. We'll move your truck up near me, when there is an opening."

"Thanks Boss. I owe you."

Couple of hours later I saw Jo wheel her truck up next to me. She set the brake and shut down the

128

engine, crawled out and climbed into mine.

"Hey, Boss, think it's gonna snow?"

"Yeah, Jo, I think it's gonna snow. It's freakin' New England!"

"So, you 'bout ready to go inside and have some dinner?"

"Sure, why not. Do it before it gets any darker and colder."

I shut the truck off and locked up. We went inside. It was warm, and crowded. We made our way to a booth near the window. Shortly, a waitress with an upper east coast accent appeared, took our order and disappeared, with a warning to not get to impatient. They were running slow.

Jo looked at me, "So, Evan, when did you see that cute little Cat girl last?"

I dropped my head, "Been a while Jo. We just don't seem to ever be going the right direction anymore."

"Fucks with your sex life, huh?"

"Yeah, if I had one," I smiled.

"Yeah, Boss, this life is hard on relationships. If you aren't awfully flexible, the conventional couple just don't have a very long life. If one or the other stays home, suspicion will arise about what the other does on those days and sometimes weeks of separation. But mostly, I think it is just the loneliness that gets to both parties. The logical pursuit is to just take your fun where you get it and be friends with you mate. That is really hard for some people to do though."

"Jo, I suppose that is what my problem is. I came from a very conservative background. I can't allow myself to think about Cat out there fuckin' around, or it would mess me up something fierce. So, therefore, I don't. But I think about it a lot."

"Evan Smith, you need to smoke more pot, and mellow out a bit. Get that rod outta your ass."

I laughed at this little half-pint girl at least five or six years my junior, giving me a life lesson in a crude but serious fashion. She was right about one thing though, I was a pretty uptight person.

Our food finally came. We ate slowly, no rush today. This was one of the parts about the truck driving world that did drive me up the wall. The hurry up and wait, the hours of sitting sometimes days, with nothing to do.

It was maddening.

"Evan, you need a driving partner. That would help you some, take some of the pressure off. Give you company, make the time go by. Life is made for sharing. And don't wait forever, life is short."

"Jo, I pulled two tours in Vietnam. You don't have to tell me anything about life being short. Believe me, I know that. As for a driving partner, yeah, I have been looking. But no one has come along, yet, that I feel good about."

"Do you want a girl or a guy?"

"I'm not particular. Just has to be the right person."

"Evan, I am going to catch a shower really quick.

Would you mind waiting for me? I'll be quick."

"Sure, go for it. I am going to make a few phone calls."

I called our office. Michelle answered the phone. She informed me that our loads were set back another 3 or 4 hours until about 8 pm the next evening. Due to the weather, she said. I could possibly understand that. The weather wasn't being that good. Spring storms are sometimes the worse.

She told me I should call Cat, she had left a message. I hung up and dialed the number given.

"Hello."

"Hi Cat."

"Hi Babe!"

"What's up?"

"Well, I am stuck in Portland again. Michelle said you are waiting on a load in Connecticut."

"I am. I wish you were here, it would be nice to

have a warm body tonight to cuddle with. Baby, it's cold outside!"

"Well, Evan Smith, you should find you one. You are a grown man, it isn't right for you to be by yourself. I love ya to death, but I don't want that, and I can't be there."

"Well, that is mighty generous of you, ma'am. But I kinda have feelings for you. That's kinda the way I am."

"And I for you, Evan. But until something happens, until we can have a life together, we simply must go on living. And I mean in every way. Make some friends of both sexes. And, if once in a while one of them gets to feel particularly good, then go for it. I love you Evan, but I would hate myself if you sat and waited for me and lost that magical zest for life that I saw in you. I mean that."

"Wow, Cat, that is a mouthful. So, how about you, are you doing the same?"

"Evan, don't worry about me. I am the same as when you met me. You liked me then, why not just keep on liking me for the way I am? And I will do the same to you."

"Cat, I need to digest this. We can talk about it later."

"OK sweetie. Now if you can, I would like to propose a vacation for us. In about a month I have to have surgery in my shoulder, and won't be able to drive for about three weeks. I want to do the surgery, then fly to Austin and convalesce with you. How does that sound?"

"No, Cat, we can't do that. If I can't hang you up and flog you, I just don't want you around. Of course, you idiot! I would love it! Jeez! What, three, four weeks?"

"Yep, pretty much."

"Oh, Hell Yes!"

We talked for another few minutes, then she had to go. About that time Jo slid back into the seat, her hair still wet from the shower and brushed straight back. She smelled good.

"You get tired of waiting? I had to wait a couple of

minutes. They didn't have my shower cleaned and ready for me when I got there."

"No ma'am, it worked out about right. I just finished also. Ready to go back to the truck?"

"Lead out Boss. I'm ready."

We returned to our trucks. Jo disappeared into her sleeper and emerged wearing what looked like flannel pj's. She fired the engine on her truck, then stepped out and back up into mine. She remarked her truck had cooled off, and she wasn't read to go to bed anyway. I told her that was fine, I enjoyed her company. She smiled and said thanks.

She reached into the pocket of her PJ and pulled out a joint, saying, "I hate to smoke alone."

I took it and took a hit, and passed it back. She took a hit, and held it for a minute, then took another. She passed it back, and I hit it again. In a few minutes the warm wonderful glow appeared. I slipped a Pink Floyd tape into the tape player. the music filled the truck, and finally all was good with the day.

Jo relaxed and pulled a brush from her pocket and started brushing her hair. I looked at her for probably the first time. She was 25. She sometimes appeared younger because of her size. She was probably 5'2", maybe 3", weighed maybe 117 or so. She had a soft voice, and could sing beautifully. I had listened to her once at the terminal singing with a radio or a tape, and was pleasantly surprised. She could drive quite good, said she had grown up in a family of truck drivers and had been driving since she was 17, though not always legally. But now she was legal, and could compete with any driver male or female.

"Hey, Jo, you don't have a sister like you who can drive, do you? In my quest for a co-driver," I added.

"Nope, I don't. But I do have a friend. If I could find her, I think you two would hit it off. I have been looking for her."

We sat enjoying the evening together, talking, listening to music, listening to the bizarre conversations over the CB. Finally, she announced her buzz was gone and she was headed for bed. I said good night, and watched her disappear into her sleeper across the way. It wasn't long until I was

136

headed for mine. The pot relaxed me and soon I was dreaming.

Sometime later I felt the truck move as someone stepped up on the running board. I raised up just in time to see Jo slide into the jump seat.

"Move over Boss. My little ass is cold. My heater isn't heating like it should. I shut the truck off. You're elected as the next heating source."

I backed into the bunk as she slid in stripped off her pj's and slid into bed with me, snuggling her butt back against me.

"Dammit girl! You weren't kidding! That is one cold ass."

She just wiggled it against me, and snuggled herself closer. I put my arm across her, intending it for comfort, but it fell over one of the firm beautiful breasts that she was endowed with. I immediately moved it down, where it fell on her firm flat tummy. Seemed like anywhere I put it, it was exciting. I lay my head back on the pillow, my face in her hair.

"Jo, what is that smell? I really like it."

"It is a combination of patchouli, vanilla and musk. I rinse it into my hair, then rub the rest of it on my body. Glad you like it."

I settled into sleep beside this beautiful woman, but the perfume, and her warm body, had the expected reaction on my body, a body that hadn't felt a woman in a few weeks.

I felt an erection rising. I was starting to become embarrassed when she said sleepily, "Oh, my. You are glad to see me, ummmm?" She rubbed her self back against me, arching her butt up, so that my dick rubbed across her naked pussy. Oh my God, this was not supposed to be happening. Still, she felt so good. She reached back and took my hand and slipped it over her breast, pushing it into my hand. My erection got bigger, she then took my hand and slipped it down between her legs. Her pubic hair was soft and downy, there wasn't much of it. She was moist and soft. I ran my fingers over her, caressing, then slipping my finger inside her. Her breath came out in a soft gasp and a sigh. She was moving her hips, back and forth and rocking sideways softly. She kept pressing herself back against me as if to impale herself on my erection, and then ..... she did. I slipped inside her. It was soft and warm, but it felt as if tiny fingers were gripping me and releasing me. I kissed her neck below her ear and put my arms about her. My hands on her breasts, she pushed and moved, arching herself, moaning softly. Suddenly, I felt her tighten about my dick, and that was all it took. I came. Oh, man, I came! It lasted for what felt like minutes, both of us moving together. She collapsed against me, and we both just melted into a heap against the wall of the sleeper.

We lay there for several minutes. Jo rolled over and kissed me.

"Thanks, Evan. That was awesome. I will always remember that as one of my best orgasms!"

We lay and talked for a while. Then I felt her hand slide down and take hold of my dick. The next thing I knew she has bent from the waist and taken me in her mouth, sliding up and down. I could feel her tongue curling around as she sucked ever so slightly. Then she sat up and threw her leg over me and sat down. She raised herself and found my now erect penis, and slide down over it. She moved now, almost hypnotically, her head back, her hair spilling around her face. She rose and fell, her lips slightly parted, soft moans escaped her lips. Her hands came to her breast, massaging them, rolling the nipples between her fingers, still rocking up and back, sometimes faster, then slower. Her right hand fell to her pussy, and slowly moved inside her and around the lips. Then she rocked hard a couple of times, lifting herself until only the head of my dick was inside her. Then faster for just a few times, her whole body stiffening, and she cried aloud, a low, moaning, almost animal cry. Then she fell forward on my chest.

She lay there for maybe a minute. She kissed me lightly, and murmured, "Thanks again. Would you mind getting dressed so I can go inside and go to the bathroom? I don't want to go by myself. Every driver in there would see it in my face, and would be after me."

"No problem. How about we get a shower, and clean up."

She nodded yes. At that time of the night there was never any waiting on showers. So we took a shower together. She still wanted to rub on me, but we finished our shower and got a cup of coffee for her and a cup of tea for me.

"So, little miss hot pants, what do we do now?"

She looked up at me. "Nothing. We do as we have done. We drive trucks. We work. We enjoy each others company. You are my boss, Jim is my guy. And if it ever happens again, we do the same. This was great, but it was a comforting in the night, nothing more."

We went back to go to bed. Before I was able to get into bed, she turned and said, "I am one orgasm ahead of you, we gotta keep this even!" She slipped out of her shirt, and knelt over me, taking my dick in her mouth. Oh, she was so good! She would look at me and smile as she worked it.

I was almost in another world, when a voice came over the CB which I hadn't turned off.

"Oh my God Driver! What I would give to be in your seat right now!"

Jo looked up and smiled sweetly. She reached up and took the mike and held it near her mouth, she said, "Driver, just imagine you are here," and slipped me back in her mouth, holding the key so he could hear every slurp, every stroke, every little moan she made. Then, in a minute or two, fireworks exploded, and just about lifted me out of my seat.

She finished me and lifted her head and whispered, "Was that good for you, Driver?"

The voice on the other end said, "Yes MA'AM! Thank you!"

I echoed that myself.

I guess my new life was born that night. It would have its highs and lows for the next few years, but the lows were not to last, and the highs were the best. Just wait and see.

I think that night was when I became a bit more selfish, perhaps cynical. If everyone else out there was just looking out for their own selves, perhaps it was time for Evan Smith to fall in line a bit. I had always been the kind of person that sometimes went overboard trying not to be unfair, or take advantage. I had the golden rule drummed into my

Southern little wooden head from the time I was old enough to understand till I was grown. A lot of my friends told me I would be a nice guy, if I would just get that stick out of my butt and loosen up a bit.

Well, OK, maybe I would now. But how? I never was a drinker, I did not like getting drunk. Some hippie friends said it had to do with my astrological sign. I was born on Sept 10th, a Virgo. But I didn't believe that crap. Still, I had always been a people watcher, and noticed the differences in personalities.

Jim made it back the next afternoon. The next morning Jo was back being her little truck driver self. No flirting, no being any more sexy than her natural self could help being. In short, professional.

We got our wagons loaded about seven pm with a delivery request for Jacksonville, Florida, the next day, ASAP. We headed out I-95 southbound. It had quit snowing, and the plows had the Jersey Pike in good shape. We made it all the way into Virginia before stopping.

As we eased our way through the crowded truck stop, a female voice came over the radio, "Little

Nitro, is that you darlin'? This is Daddies Girl!"

Jo's voice came back, "Sweetie! How are you? Come inside, we gotta boogie. Want'a squeeze your cute body though. Hey, have you seen Shadow?"

"Nitro, catch ya in a short short, inside. 10-4."

"Roger that darlin'."

We went inside a hit the restrooms first, then restaurant for an early breakfast. We hadn't eaten since mid afternoon, so everyone was hungry. We had just ordered our food, when a tall, redheaded girl, slid into my booth beside me, across from Jim and Jo. Jo said, "Mandy, meet my boss Evan. Evan, Mandy." I turned and shook hands with her. As we ate, the girls rattled on a mile a minute, trying to catch up on past news. Jo asked about the person she had referred to as Shadow.

"Sweetie, Shadow is working for a company up in Missouri. She isn't real happy. The equipment sucks, and the money isn't real good either. She isn't real happy."

"Good, Boss. Give Mandy one of your cards.

Mandy, get word to her and tell her to call our terminal. Evan is looking for a co-driver. I think they would match really good."

Mandy agreed to do it and we were soon on the road again. Later that afternoon, we unloaded our wagons in Jacksonville. We already had orders for two loads over near Tampa, one a load of orange juice for Jo and Jim, and the other a load of tomatoes for me. The OJ was taking them to Houston, and me to Colorado Springs.

I loaded a day later, and headed out on the long drive to Colorado. I had to check the tomatoes every so often and vent the trailer occasionally. Some produce is a real pain in the butt to haul. I took I-10 over to Mississippi, north on I-55 up to Memphis, then headed across I-40. I figured keeping south of I-70 would keep me in better weather. I stopped in Little Rock to catch up on some much needed rest. I called Michelle to give her my position. She informed me she had a number for me to call, from a young lady named Sheryl, about a job. I took the number, and as soon as we had finished our business I called her. A quiet female voice answered.

"Hello?"

"Is this Sheryl? This is Evan Smith."

"Oh yes, Mr. Smith! A friend of mine name of Mandy said you were in the market for a driver."

"Yes, I am. But no Mr. Smith, just Evan will do. I actually am looking for someone to run team with me. I have got a lot of business, and I am running myself ragged trying to be a team of one myself. One of my drivers, Jo, recommended you very highly. Would you mind telling me a little about yourself and your experience?"

We talked for about an half hour, and she told me about her experience and needs. I told her I was willing to give her a chance, and if it didn't work out, I would help her re-situate herself. She said that was fair enough. She asked where I was, and where I was headed at the moment. I told her I was in Little Rock headed for Colorado. She said that would be pretty easy. She had quit her job about a week ago, and was in Big Cabin, Oklahoma with a friend and she could meet me the next day at the truck stop on the west side of Okie City. Said when I get there, to give a yell for Shadow.

I agreed. I showered and shaved and got about 5 hours of sleep before heading westbound. About 11 the next morning I passed through Okie City. As I approached a truck stop, I keyed my mike and said, "Shadow, you out there?"

Quick as a wink, she answered. "That you Evan?"

"10-4."

"Come around to the back row look for a brown Freightliner. Lights will be on."

"Roger that."

I eased around back and pulled up beside the Freightliner. I looked over and saw a very attractive young woman sitting in the jump seat. She raised her hand for a moment, then opened her door and stepped out. Sheryl was about 5'7", maybe 5'8" and weighed maybe a 125 to 130. She had dark hair. Her look made you think there might be Latin or Native American blood in her heritage somewhere. She was soft-spoken, but very direct, and seemed to be a no nonsense girl. I stepped down and introduced myself.

"Hi, I'm Evan."

"Hi Evan, I am Sheryl."

"Well Sheryl, if you are ready to start a new gig, I am ready. Do you have any baggage?"

"A couple."

She reached into the side door of the Freightliner and pulled a couple of soft suitcases out and a large purse type bag.

"This too much?"

"Looks good too me." I opened the side door on the sleeper and said, "You can stow it in here, till we have time to square it away."

She nodded agreement, and put her gear on board. Then she turned to the guy in the Freightliner and said, "Thanks, Johnny. I'll see you somewhere!"

He threw her a half salute.

I turned to her and said, "You're driving. Make yourself comfortable." By the time I had reached the other side of the rig and climbed in, she had settled in, adjusted her seat, and asked me to tip the passenger side mirror in just a scooch. I did that.

She slipped the tranny into low and eased down the back row and out around the driveway, turned onto the street to the overpass, and in a few minutes had finished the pattern and we were westbound. I slid back in the jump seat and watched her mannerisms as she drove.

"Sheryl, looks like you have done this at least a couple of times."

"Thanks. Driving has always seemed natural to me from the very first. I love the rhythm of the shifting, the movement of a truck under a load, the power. I can drive for hours and not get bored or tired. Actually, even when I am tired as well."

"Well, if this is going to be a long time arrangement, lets play a game. I always did this in Vietnam when I got a replacement, or a new guy, in my platoon. Start out with your pet peeves, and list them from most disliked to bearable."

She laughed. "You really want to know? What if some of them are your habits?"

"Then when you are finished, I will tell you mine, and we will compare. Yours first."

"OK. Guys that think because I run team with them, I have to fuck them."

"No problem. Now my first one. Girls that drive for me that think because they work for me, I have to fuck them."

She laughed. "You asshole! I like you all ready!

"Number two. Co-drivers that don't bathe regularly."

"Daily, at least. More if necessary," I added.

"I want my share of hours to be equal, not all nights, or all bad road, or all city."

"That's fair," I added. "What else?"

"Dunno. How about we think on it some? I think I

have a good feeling about this anyway."

"Me too."

"Me too," Sheryl echoed.

"Stop at the Petro in Amarillo. I want to fuel and eat before we head north. I am going to take a quick nap now."

"Gotcha Boss, will do."

"Pet Peeve Number 3. Don't call me boss!"

She smiled and gave me a thumbs up.

I dozed quickly, and in what felt like minutes later we were entering the Petro. I had showered in Little Rock that morning, but I was hungry. I told my new co-driver if she felt the need to shower, the time was hers. She said she was good, so we ate dinner and talked.

After eating, she asked, "Evan, do you smoke pot?"

I laughed, "Yeah, do you?"

She nodded yes.

"How about when you drive?"

"Occasionally."

"Wow, that is a load off my mind. Now mind you, I am no stoner, but it keeps me thinking and alleviates the boredom. You can watch me drive after I have smoked and if you don't feel comfortable you let me know. Ok?"

"Fair enough. Trust is a big thing between team members."

"Exactly, Evan. I will do everything I can to earn your trust."

"And I will do likewise, partner!" I stuck out my hand, she took it and shook it.

"Ok, let's get these tomatoes to Colorado!"

We left Amarillo heading north up US 287. About 45 miles up the road was the little town of Dumas, Texas. We turned west on US 87, out through

Hartley, then Dalhart, Texline, and Clayton, New Mexico. By then it was a full moon. The mountains around us were all volcanic in nature, the moon lit up the countryside. Soon we passed the Capulin Volcano, and then Raton. We started our climb up Raton Pass and over the line into Colorado. I always loved this drive and on a full moon night, with my new friend by my side, it was a memorable experience. We smoked a joint and chatted the whole trip, telling stories from our lives, learning about each other, our likes and dislikes. Most married couples never spend the time together that a set of team drivers does. We stopped at the 110 mile marker on I-25, at the Piñon Truck stop.

Our delivery time was 3 hours away, and we were only 30 minutes from it. I decided I wanted to lay down for a while, so I crawled into the bunk and lay down. Sheryl followed me but she slipped out of her jeans before we lay down. Sleeper beds are not real large, so we wound up quite close. She turned to face me.

"Evan, I want to feel relaxed with you. I am not saying I will never have sex with you, because I probably will, but first I just want to learn to be comfortable with you, and yet not make you

154

uncomfortable."

I smiled and put my finger on the tip of her nose and said, "Sounds like a perfect relationship. Now shut up and go to sleep. I set the alarm for two hours."

She kissed me a short quick kiss and said, "Ok, Boss!" And turned over and we slept.

Two hours later I awoke to find this pretty lady still sleeping snuggled against me. I nudged her in the back and said, "Ok, driver, time to earn your pay, instead of sleeping with the boss."

She laughed and jumped up and pulled her jeans on. "Oh, My! I gotta go pee so bad! I'll catch you inside." She pulled her boots on as she went out the door. I was not far behind her.

We had a good breakfast at the Piñon. I always enjoyed stopping there. When we got back to the truck Sheryl went immediately to the driver's door without being asked. She stopped and turned.
"So, Evan, do you trust me enough to have me a set of keys made yet?"

I laughed, "Yep, just as soon as we get this load off we will find a hardware store. Better yet, we will run into the Springs and go to the dealer. There are a couple of things I need fixed anyway."

She gave me a thumbs up and I unlocked the door. I was impressed watching this young woman handle the rig through the streets and backing into the dock. She was professional in every way. I knew I had made a good decision. After the trip to the Kenworth dealer in Colorado Springs, I called Michelle. She said she thought she had a load out of Denver, but hadn't firmed it up. But we should probably go on up there and hang out. By then it was late afternoon. We headed north up I-25 to I-70. Exiting to the right, we took the ramp westbound. We got off at exit 266 and found the entrance to the 76 truck stop and idled back to the back row, in search of a parking place. Sheryl found one and eased the 45 footer back into place. She set the brakes and cut the engine, and said, "Ok, what next?"

I said, "Well, ma'am, lets go get ourselves all prettied up. There is an Italian restaurant about a mile up the street. I propose to take you to dinner, to celebrate our new partnership!"

156

She smiled, "I love Italian!"

We went in to get a shower, and after a short wait the attendant informed us that if we were a couple there was a shower available that we could have.

Sheryl spoke up quickly. "Yeah, we're a couple!"

I looked at her questioningly. She smiled and said, "C'mon, darling, people are waiting!"

We entered the shower. She said, "Don't take this for more than it is. I am not a prude. I don't mind nudity, I hope you don't either. I like sleeping nude, I like being nude. It doesn't mean I am going to fuck you, every time we get nude."

I said, "You know what? The longer I know you, the more I like you. It is going to be so easy to work with you. Southeast Asia pretty much took the modest out of my system."

We stripped and stepped into the shower together. She had a gorgeous body, I had to give her that. We soaped and each did our own thing, taking turns under the flow of water. After I had finished I said, "Need your back washed?" She turned her back to me and I soaped and washed her back with a washcloth. I finished and stepped out and dried myself. I shaved where I needed and trimmed a few places, then dressed and slipped into my boots. I told her I would be outside.

I stepped out into the hall and walked down to the TV room and stood watching the news while I waited. The news was a still on the Arab oil embargo, and the effects on fuel prices. There had been some events on the east coast where truckers were running, when Unions had ordered shutdowns. Drivers were shot at, bricks were thrown off overpasses. As yet, we hadn't had any problems yet. Oh, yes, the gas lines at service stations. But like everything else, America adapted. It was hard to imagine oil in just a matter of days jumping from $3 a barrel to $12 a barrel. How would we ever recover from it?

About that time I felt a hand on my arm. I turned, and there before me was Sheryl, dressed to kill. Or at least as a driver could go. She was wearing just enough makeup to accent her face. She was stunning.

"Ok, Boss. Will this do for a dinner date?"

"Only if you never call me boss again!"

"Ok, Partner," she smiled.

We took our bags and laundry to the truck and stowed them, then walked back to the entrance. I dialed the number for a yellow cab that someone had stuck on the wall. I gave our name and where we were. By the time I hang up and walked outside, the cab was pulling up to the door. It was a short ride down the street to the restaurant.

Vincinza's was an Italian Bakery and Restaurant in Wheat Ridge, Colorado. Frenchy had taken me there a few times. The smells had you salivating before your food ever arrived.

"Oh, God! Have we transported to Jersey?" was all Sheryl could say.

We ordered, each picking something different. I had a salad with a bread you dipped in a vinegar wine sauce and a pasta dish with Alfredo sauce. After the main course we went and picked desserts from the bakery. And this where it got dangerous.

There were just too many, so we chose too many. But decided they would make good munchies after a joint later!

The owner and his wife remembered me from being there with Frenchy, so they came and inquired to his whereabouts. I had to tell them he had passed. The lady turned quickly away and wiped an eye as she left. I wondered if I would ever get everyone of his friends told.

Back to the truck stop where we called Michelle. Still no confirmation, so we headed out to our large car. We went back into the sleeper and Sheryl slipped out of her tight jeans, and nice shirt and put on something more comfortable.

I slid out to the driver's seat and put a tape in the player. The spring air was still cold in the Rocky Mountains, so I started the engine and turned the heater on low. Sheryl came out. She handed me an already lit joint. I took a hit and returned it. We took a couple more and settled back as the stars came out over the mountaintop to the west of us.

The speed limits of the '70s dropped to 55 mph nationwide as a result of the alleged fuel shortages.

The motoring public hated it, and particularly the over the road truck driver. If your pay was based on mileage, as it was in most cases, or sometimes percentages, then it was a direct pay cut. Before that you could log up to something over 700 miles in a 10 hour period. Afterward, it would be difficult to log 500. So drivers ran more than one log book. Team driving made the venture a bit more lucrative, especially man and wife teams. It also really brought the CB radio in as a necessary piece of truck equipment. Drivers gave other drivers Bear reports. It was not unusual to hear over the radio something to the effect "West bound, full grown in the median at the 223", or "Smoky Bear, rolling southbound at the 119". Some Bears hated the radios; some Smokey's got CBs of their own and listened in. Some recognized the usefulness of the CB's for reporting dangers on the roadways, accidents, and etc. But the point is, everyone was guilty of speeding. It was necessary for productivity for truckers. Cops started using radar to catch truckers, truckers started using radar detectors to keep from being caught. Some drivers even went as far as to install brake light cut off switches, so if they met a bear, they could nail their brakes without the bear seeing their brake lights light up.

My partner and I picked up our load next morning at the yard of a Mountain Bell contractor in Arvada, bound for Phoenix. We loaded and headed up through Morrison over US285. We topped Kenosha Pass in time to see a large herd of elk gallop off into the aspens. We dropped down across South Park, the air was fresh and clean up here. We rolled past Fairplay, over Trout Creek Pass and down through Johnson's corner, past Poncha Springs and Salida, up Poncha Pass, and across the San Luis Valley. Deep in the southwest we could see the San Juan Mountains, almost a hundred miles away. By afternoon we found ourselves motoring up Wolf Creek Pass behind two loaded tankers. The drivers were busy in a conversation. I got interested and turned the radio up, in time to hear one of the drivers telling about an experience that he had on this mountain pass.

"Driver, I wanna tell you, this got really serious. I was a couple of miles further up here ahead of us now, almost to the snow shed, when an avalanche came down in front of me. I stopped my truck and set the brakes. About that time, about 200 yards behind me, another came down, closing the road behind me. I got out and looked up the mountain above me. I was happy to see that I didn't have

162

much buildup above me, figured I was safe where I was. Which was good thing, cause I damn sure wasn't going anywhere!

"I got on my radio and yelled for a Smokey, or anyone else. No answer! So about every 30 minutes or so I would give a yell. After about 2 hours or so, somebody came back to me. Said he had a Smokey there and would get him to come talk to me. He did. Mr. Smokey said it would be the next day before they could get the road open. Driver, I sat up there on that mountain for 24 hours before they got a front loader down there and got that road open! Well, it was a damn good thing I always carry food with me. 'Course, I had plenty of fuel to keep warm, wudda been nice if would I had a bedroom, though, and a nice little beaver to keep me company. It was a long night."

"I hear that, Driver. Now, I gotta tell you one. I had took me a load of gas over to Rifle one day. Got unload about dark, and had made it back to Vail. I was about halfway up Vail, it was snowin' so hard you could barely see past your hood. All of a sudden the car in front of me was stopped. 'Bout that time, somebody said on the radio that the uphill side on the east bound was closed. They said it would be hours. I set my brakes and got out and put a couple of wheel chocks in place, just for safety. As I was doing that I looked back and saw a little four-wheeler setting behind my trailer. I walked back, and pecked on the window. This really pretty girl rolled the window down. I told her, 'Darlin', I just wanted you to know, that the road is shut down up ahead. Probably for the rest of the night.' She replied that was a problem, as she was very low on gas. I did what any red blooded truck driver would do. I invited her up to join me. She did. Turns out she was college girl going to Boulder. She had some soft drinks and chips and stuff and I had some other stuff. But the main thing, she had about a quarter of some really good weed! So we sat all night and smoked and ate, and listened to music and talked. No hanky-panky, Driver, although it would have been nice. She had a sweet little body. Finally, just before dawn we fell asleep. When we woke up, the plows were opening the road.

"She gave me her number, and we went out a few times. About six month later, we got married. We have been married a year now, and have a baby on the way. Luckiest blizzard that ever blew down a mountain pass!"

I listened to these stories, then the idea came to me. I remembered the stories at Frenchy's wake. I would write these stories down, this was good stuff! At some point in the future, I might have enough to fill a book! It had not been but a short while since I had entered the trucking world. I had no idea of the lifestyle, and daily activities, of these remarkable people. They were the modern day cowboys, the modern day pioneers, or mountain men.

But how to do this? I couldn't write while I was driving. I told Sheryl of my thoughts. Her answer, "Tape it." Write it later. Of course! The next day, after we unloaded, I found a Radio Shack and bought me a tape recorder and several tapes. I was ready.

We headed over to the truck stop on Black Canyon Highway, and lo and behold, there was Jim and Jo sitting at the fuel Islands.

Jo and Sheryl were immediately wrapped up in each others arms, hugging and kissing, and generally making a delicious spectacle of themselves. We got ourselves situated and parked, and went down the street to find a decent restaurant.

We had a meal and caught up on business. We went back to our trucks, Sheryl and Jo headed for Jo's truck and Jim came and sat with me and we visited for several hours. Finally, the girls showed up, looking very satisfied with themselves. We smoked a little weed and finally about 11 pm or so Jim and Jo went back to their rig. Next morning Michelle had us loads. This time we switched trailers with Jim and Jo. We gave them our reefer, and we took their double drop lowboy. Jim and Jo went to pick up a load of produce going to Houston. Sheryl and I were deadheading to Edwards Air Force Base, north of L.A. in Antelope Valley to pick up a load going to New York.

We arrived late in the evening and stopped at a little Pub to have some food. Sheryl had a beer and she was talking to a guy in the bar and came back to me later, saying that this guy can get some really good weed, did I want a quarter? I said yeah, sure. We gave him our $35 bucks and he left. We waited and waited and played pool and waited. About two hours later, I told Sheryl, "I think the $35 has found a new home." We had just decided to go back to our truck and crash when the guy walked back in the door. Oh, well, I suppose I can be wrong. We went out to the truck and Sheryl rolled one up, took a hit and offered to him. He declined, "Oh, no, I don't smoke!" Oh, shit, I could just about see the cops appearing. But he was telling the truth. We thanked him and he left, and we found a place for the night. Well, the reason I am telling you the story is to tell you about this weed. It turned out to be Maui Waui, if anyone knows about that stuff. We were tired and smoked very little and went right to sleep, not realizing how potent it was.

We arrived at Edwards about nine. Our load was a passenger loading ramp for aircraft, and an assortment of crates. We were loaded in an hour and headed east, for an Air Force Base near Blythesville, Arkansas. And listen to this... they gave us four days to do it. Not good news to a team, especially after such a long deadhead to get it. But sometimes that is the way the cookie crumbles. We decided to take I-40 to Little Rock, and up to Blythesville.

That afternoon found us just outside of Kingman, Arizona. We decided to call it a day.

After the ritual of fuel food showers and smoke, we found ourselves in an almost empty truck stop. Nothing even on the radio for entertainment. I took out my spiral note pad and started to write, starting with my memories of my early days with Frenchy and the stories he told. I asked Sheryl if she had any truck driving stories. She smiled.

"Sure, but they wouldn't be for little children to read!"

I told her that probably wouldn't matter, cause I didn't see this coming out like a children s book anyway.

She said she would tell me some of them as she remembered a good one ever so often.

One she told me stands out. A couple of friends of hers were rolling westbound over about Grand Island, Nebraska one night, when the red lights came on behind them. The only reason, they had a light not working. Jerry, the dude, evidently didn't make an impression on the trooper, so they searched the truck. They found a tiny trace of crank in a little bag, so they impounded the truck. They took the couple to the crossbar hotel, where they

168

spent the weekend. After they had made bail, they left the county.

The woman, we'll call her Sue, started laughing. They had taken her purse. When she would ask for something out of it, they would hand it back, she would take what was needed, then hand it back to them.

She did that the whole weekend, seems like. She had a quarter-ounce of pot in a baggie in her purse the whole time. Everyone got a good laugh about that!

The weed we had purchased in California turned out to be totally mind numbing. The best I had ever smoked since the Black Vietnamese Pot. We smoked a joint, and I stretched out in the bunk to write. Sheryl came back and took off all her clothes.

"Evan, I hate wearing clothes on my off hours. I hope you can deal with this."

I had removed my shirt and jeans and was just wearing my briefs.

"Sheryl, we have to be comfortable. I will deal

with it. After all, you are not hard to look at, ever."

She sat on the bunk beside me. "Those scars from Vietnam?"

"Yes ma'am."

"You don't talk about that much."

"It is not always a pleasant subject to talk about."

"I understand. My cousin was there. He doesn't talk much either."

The weed was just about mesmerizing. I put my notebook up and lay back and closed my eyes. Seconds later, Sheryl lay down beside me, facing me.

"Wow, this stuff is really good isn't it?" she asked.

"OH, Yeah!" I replied, "I am not sure I could drive on it very well."

She laughed, "Lucky, you are not driving, huh?"

She kept laughing and pretty soon got me started.

170

She put her arms round me and hugged herself against me still giggling. I returned the hug.

She stooped laughing, and lifted her head and kissed me lightly on the lips, very soft and lingering, as if she was trying to taste me. I looked at her, and slipped my arm around her back and lifted her body toward me, and just enjoyed the softness of her lips and the sweetness of her breath. She relaxed away from for a second, and I let my arm relax from her. She reached out and touched my face with her hand, then let it slide down off my shoulder to my chest. She ran her fingers across my chest, and along my stomach.

She then came forward again and kissed me, a bit more intensely than before, but nevertheless, still softly. I stroked her back and her hair as I held her to me. Her leg curled about my leg pulling her body tightly against me. By now, I was as excited as she seemed to be. I wanted her. I wanted to be as close to her as I could get.

I reached to the waistband of my briefs and shoved them down, and off. She moved herself against me; her hand went down to my penis. She enveloped it with her hand, stroked it a couple of times, then rolled up on top of me spreading her legs and taking me inside her. She lowered herself against me and went back to kissing me and tasting with her tongue. I felt like I never wanted this to stop. Her body was firm and hard from work and youth, but the soft, velvety-ness of her skin was amazing. It didn't take long for either of us. I felt her body tensing, tightening, and it brought me to the end of my journey as well. We both climaxed at once, thoroughly, but quietly.

She did not move, but lay there, with me inside of her, holding me close to her, her lips still only an inch from mine, her head on my shoulder, her eyes closed. Her breath, still soft and sweet, slowed, and her heartbeat returned to normal.

She opened her eyes. I looked at her. She smiled a little smile. She looked at me and said, "That was very good, Boss."

I slapped her bare ass, "I told you about that!"

She smiled again.

"I wasn't sure about this Evan, but I like you. I think we have a good thing going. The pot put me in the mood, and I am glad it did. I told you I prefer girls, but I occasionally like the attentions of a man as well. This was good. I don't want it to change anything in our relationship."

"Sheryl, I promise, from my end it won't. I appreciate you sharing this with me. It was a sweet experience, and I will always remember it."

Three days later we were unloading the big load at Blythesville AFB, Arkansas.

Our jobs took us on an unending circuit around the U.S. We went to bed some place different, and woke up in another state. The life really appealed to me. And with Sheryl as a partner, it became quite carefree. We made a point to never get in each others way. When she found a girl that appealed to her, she did her thing. When we got out to the west coast once, and I was able to connect with Cat, she found other activities. She and Cat hit it off immediately though, and one summer day the three of us were able to go spend a day at the beach together. They talked a lot to each other. I believe they would have become good friends, but Cat and I were drifting part. Not because we didn't care for each other, we did, but we just seemed to evolve away from one another. We both seemed to be sad, but we couldn't find an answer. I sure it happened a lot with OTR drivers and stay at home wives or husbands as well. The open road is a subtle thief. It steals one's attentions, and never gives them back. It is a lonely life for those that go it alone. But there are some who like it that way. There has always been the loners. They have been called explorers, gypsies, cowboys, mountain men. But the truth of the matter is, they just have to see what is on the other side of the mountain, or on the other side of the forest.

And then, there are the trucks. When one crawls up in the drivers seat of a big rig, and heads off

174

down the highway, the comfort of being in control of that giant beast weighing in at 40 ton, that being in control of that kind of power and making it go where you choose, there's something about that. After you become proficient, then, comes the feeling of comradeship and pride when you wheel your rig into a parking spot at a big truck stop. That feeling of *Esprit de Corps,* while joining the battalions of other truckers, and the odd kind of camp life that comes with it. Whereas all truck drivers fit in the mold that has been created for all truck drivers, they each have different characteristics. The freight haulers, usually short haul, local drivers, rock haulers, with both end dumps and belly dumps, the tanker drivers, with fuel and chemicals, etc. Then the portable parking lots, hauling new cars and trucks. The OTR long haul, mostly dry boxes, refers, and flatbeds. And then the heavy haul, with the big oversize and over-weight stuff - each require separate training, even in the way they drive the trucks. Different techniques for different jobs.

In the 1960's and early '70's for sure, and even on into the late '70's, the trucking world was much more bonded. As the '80's came around and it grew so much, it became a wilder, more profane society.

A lot of the truck stops became actually dangerous at times. This was especially true for the women who worked in the industry.

One afternoon in late '74, I got a really good truck driving story from an unexpected source. Someone I met once years before.

We had picked up a load of copper wire rolls at the Hayden mine in Arizona, and went down the road a few miles to the little town of Mammoth, on the San Pedro River. It was hot - hot only as Arizona seems to get. We stopped at a little Service Station and garage and convenience store combination.

There was a blue Kenworth Conventional over on the side, with someone working on the tires.

We had gone in and got us a snack and a Dr. Pepper, when in walked a young man in jeans and western shirt and cowboy hat. Something about him looked familiar. He looked at me, and said, "Don't I know you? I am Larry Murley."

"Hi, Larry. Evan Smith. This is Sheryl. You do look familiar."

I think we both recognized each other at the same time.

"OH, YEAH! We met in Phoenix on bikes, we had tacos together," he exclaimed.

"You are right, I remember," I answered.

We talked together for a few minutes and ate our snacks. I told him about my induction into the word of trucking. We were about ready to hit the road, when he said, "Evan, if you have a minute, I would like to tell you a story about my latest trucking experience. I just finished something that scared the piss outta me, and I gotta tell someone."

I thought for a moment, then said, "Wait just a minute. I have started recording stories, let me get my recorder." So I got it out and this is the story Larry told me that day in Arizona in 1974.

"Evan, the owner of my company dispatched me with a load of pipe to a mine up there," he pointed to the dark range of mountains to the north.

"I arrived here early this morning, and went up that road. It's pretty rough. I went up a few miles, then I reached a point and it turned slightly to the right. As I turned I approached the edge of a canyon, I slowed to a stop, then edged forward. All I could see was down and darkness. Then I looked to my left, and there was the road running along the side of the canyon. I had been warned it was dangerous, but Holy Shit Batman! So I dropped the tranny over into low and edged on over till I could see the curve to the left. Hooray, I made it! Then down the grade - and I do mean grade! I would bet it was close to 10%.

"As I reached the next turn to the right, I edged my steering axle over to the left as far as it would go, I watched my right mirror as the trailer wheels came closer and closer to the edge. It soon became apparent that I would not make it, the wheels would fall off into the canyon. I stopped. I slipped the tranny into reverse and let out on the clutch. The drivers slipped a bit in the loose gravel, but slowly I backed back up the road and got my trailer tires over to the left side as far as I could. Then I proceeded again. I made it around the curve, however, the outer wheels were hanging off in the air as I went around. I had three more curves that were somewhat like that before I reached the bottom. I reached the mine, and they unloaded the

178

pipe. As I was sitting there, I noticed all their vehicles were four-wheel drive. I asked the foreman if anyone had ever run off that road coming down. His answer, a cheery, 'Naw, not yet.'

"My boss had told me that when I come back out of the mine to make sure my power divider was locked in. As the foreman signed the bills, he looked at me and said, "Make sure you have your power divider locked in." I nodded Ok.

I made it okay coming back up the narrow windy road. I dragged the trailer around the sharp curves, as I approached the end of the road, I kept having to shift down. I finally dropped two gears and went into second. As I climbed up and out of the canyon, all eight tires were spinning for the lat 30 feet. I was getting really worried when I cleared the top. I stopped and got out, and I had two tires flat, one on each side of the drivers. That is what they were doing when you arrived."

I clicked the recorder off.

"Damn, Larry, that is quite a tale. Glad you made it."

"Well, I tell you Evan, I am not going to ever do that again. I will never go back to that mine."

We visited a few minutes more, then said goodbye and headed our different directions. I thought it interesting. How many aspects, and how many talents were brought into play by the drivers in their daily duties? It also came to mind how the same people keep popping up in different places on the road.

In '76, I traded the KW in on a Pete. I bought a new Mercury sleeper for it. I had it made with a larger bed than most trucks, for those times we both needed to sleep at the same time. At the same time they did a custom fit so that it was a walk-in from the cab.

Our new rig required a trip to Southern California. We picked up a load of grapefruit out of Tempe, Arizona, and scooted off westbound on old US 80. Just 'bout two or three miles west of Buckeye, we hung a right and caught I-10 out across the desert. Out past Tonopah, and Harquahala Valley the road rolled flat and straight. My memories went back to the first time on the Harley, when I had gone through Wickenberg and Aguila and Salome. It

180

seemed like yesterday, and half a lifetime at the same time. So much had happened. One never knows what occurs, in that momentary lapse of time, between dim lights and bright lights, when you hit that button. Somewhere, in that nano second, another universe is created. Such is time!

We pulled into the Ontario 76 about nine that evening. The CB radio was alive with people looking for smokin' dope, and commercial beavers. It was always a rowdy truck stop.

We sat back and listened to the radio for a few minutes, then decided to get a bite to eat. We took our shower bags inside just in case, but really had no hopes of getting a shower.

Dinner was only mediocre. We were fast getting into a habit of finding other restaurants. There were a few truck stops that had good food, but it was getting to be a rare thing.

Dinner done, and no showers, we went back to the rig.

As we approached our truck, a female voice yelled, "Shadow! Hey, Shadow! Wait, wait for me!"

We stopped and turned. A short Hispanic girl, in her mid twenties, came running up and grabbed Sheryl in her arms and hugged her.

"Mary! So good to see you, sweetie! Where you been?" Sheryl asked.

"I'm running team with a guy. I just have a minute, we gotta appointment to unload downtown Shaky at two am."

"Yeah, our time is at 4 or 4:30. Mary, this is Evan. Evan, Mary Montoya. She is a special friend."

I nodded hello and shook her hand.

"Sheryl, we are coming back after we unload. Any chance we can get together?"

"Dunno, maybe." She looked at me. I nodded yes.

"Probably sometime tomorrow afternoon. We are loading in Corvina."

"Oh, sweetie! I have missed you! I hope so, I gotta go now. I will look for you!" She turned to run away.

As she did, Sheryl called to her.

"Mary! Evan is trading his truck tomorrow morning look for a big, black Pete, with a big sleeper. Either yell for me or Wind Walker, Ok?"

Mary turned and ran backwards, for a couple of steps, and blew a kiss back at us.

We got in the truck, and I remarked, "Nice lady. Known her long?"

"Long enough, Evan. I just love her! If we connect, I may want some alone time, if it is Ok. Not that you have to leave the truck, just sleeper time."

I grinned, "Oh, that close a friend, huh? Not a problem. I'll just go away and pout, Ok?"

"Naw, you can just polish your new tanks or wheels or shine your dash, or tune your radio, or somethin' like that. She is just an awesome lover, and so passionate, you would probably love her too."

"Anyway, Sheryl, the space is yours. You know that."

She leaned over and kissed me, "You're the best!"

Next morning early we kicked off the grapefruit and rolled out to the Pete dealer.

Sitting in the drive to one side was our new ride. The black Pete Hood, with Mercury sleeper mounted painted the same. Shiny polished aluminum wheels, twin chrome stacks, chrome air cleaners, two black CB antennas mounted on the mirrors. It was gorgeous.

Sheryl looked and said, "Oh My God! Is that it?"

"That's it, Love."

We pulled our trailer over to a side lot for trailers and parked and walked to the new truck.

As we approached, a salesman approached.

"Are you Evan? I am Joe Black."

"Yep, I'm Evan. Good to meet you Joe. This is my partner, Sheryl."

They shook hands.

Joe asked, "Ready to check it out?"

"You bet!"

The rest of the morning and till about mid afternoon were spent moving from one to the other. We were briefed on service and technical points by the shop foreman. And getting our CB radio installed. By two pm we were hooked to our new trailer, and ready to go pick up our next load.

I looked over a Sheryl. She had a big smile on her face. Such a pretty face, especially lit up with a smile.

I said, "What?"

She said, "This is so cool! I have never driven a totally new truck, especially one as cool as this!"

I thought for a minute. "So, get your sweet little ass over here in the driver's seat. You just earned the maiden voyage."

She gasped, and put her hand over her heart.

"No! Really? It's your truck! No shit? I won't argue! God, I love you! I am not going to argue!"

And here she came. I stepped back into the edge of the sleeper and let her pass and settle into the seat. She fired the engine, slipped the tranny into second, cleared the brake, and eased down the drive, passed the waving salesmen and a couple of mechanics that had helped. She had the proudest look on her face. She looked over and smiled, then her eyes went back to the road.

Sometimes it is the smallest things that give the most pleasure. And I am not talking about her driving, although I know she loved it. But to me, to see her enjoy it, was far more pleasurable than it would to have drove it out my self.

We found the little warehouse, and was shortly loaded with all kinds of kitchen chemicals, detergents, soaps, and other household cleaning items bound for Krogers in Houston.

We headed back out to the 76, and arrived just at dark. We headed in and lucked out and got much needed showers. I weighed our wagon and found it was a bit heavy on the nose, but still legal, so I only filled with 150 gallons of fuel. California fuel was always expensive anyway.

We had found a spot back on the back row, where traffic seemed to be lighter. We fired up a joint, and toasted our new ride, and was listening to music on the new stereo, which had speakers wired into the sleeper. We had decided this would be a pleasurable few hundred thousand miles. About that time, the CB, asked, "Shadow, you there?"

"Yeah, Mary!" Sheryl told her our location.

Mary remarked they had just pulled in, and she was headed for the showers, and some food, but would be over in an hour or so.
"Roger that," Sheryl said.

Down the row, two guys were pushing each other around. I thought about intervening, then decided it wasn't my business. There was some yelling and posturing, but it soon went away.

Another rig went by. It had a lot of extra lights along the running board and bottom of the sleeper. I thought to myself, "That looks nice, maybe I will do that." I had been seeing trucks and trailers with extra lights, and I thought it was a good idea. It seemed to be for the most part a southern USA thing, didn't see it much up north.

A cop circled through, stopping briefly where all the shouting was going on, then left.

Sheryl came up front.

"Evan, have I have died and gone to heaven? This bed is great!"

About that time, Mary's head popped up at the window.

"Hi guys," she drawled smoothly, "Need any commercial company?"

Sheryl laughed and replied, "Get your cute little ass in here!"

In a minute, both the girls were in the sleeper.

I glanced back at one point. All I could see was naked girl skin, so I managed to keep my eyes forward.

About a half an hour later Sheryl called, "Evan, come back here."

I turned and squatted in the doorway in front of the bed.

The bed was decorated in tanned girl bodies. there was Sheryl's tawny dark skinned and dark hair, with her long legged slender frame lying in front of her was Mary, much shorter, a bit darker, busty, very full blown, very well proportioned, and well rounded. It was a very exotic setting. I was a bit ill at ease, but still admiring them, when Sheryl said.
"Evan, Mary has a present. But I wanted to ask you first."

Mary said, "Evan, I have about two lines of coke for each of us, if it would be alright?"

I looked at them, and said, "Sure, we have all night for it too get out of our system. I have had some in the past, I like it."

She quickly pulled a mirror out her bag and laid out the lines. Handing me a soda straw, she offered me first. I took the mirror and the straw and quickly snorted my share. She next laid out Sheryl's and she took her's as quickly, then Mary finished the tasty little treat up. As she did, Sheryl lit a joint and passed it to me. My blood was already rushing, and my energy was climbing. My nose felt dry and numb, but a good numb. The pot seemed to enhance the moment. Soon we were rattling a mile a minute, each talking at the same time. I thought for a moment, "What an awesome spot to be in, this needs to be recorded," when there came a lull in the conversation.

Mary said, "Evan, Sheryl has been telling me how good you are to her and how fairly you treat her. She told me about you letting her drive your new truck before you even had a chance to drive it. That is just too cool for words! She means a lot to me. So we talked, and you have this new ride, and you are a good guy, so we want to give you a house warming party. So, Evan, *Happy New Truck Day!*"

With that she turned and put her arms around my neck and kissed me warn and hard. She toyed with my lips with her tongue. At the same time I felt Sheryl's arms around me. The girls turned me around and rolled me back on the bed and started undressing me. In seconds I was as bare as the day I was born.

Then they were on top and each side of me, kissing me each in turn, kissing my chest, running their hands over me. The coke had me erect already. I felt their hands rubbing my penis, both at the same time. Oh, God, what had I ever done to deserve this! Then Mary slid down my chest and across my stomach, and I felt her take me in her mouth. I felt like I was floating in air. I put my hands on each side of Sheryl's waist and lifted her up, until I could kiss her breast and lick the tight little nipples. That was okay for a moment, then I wanted more. I could feel Mary licking and sucking me and sliding me in and out of her mouth. I felt suspended in time. I lifted Sheryl up again and kissed my way across he tight tummy higher and higher until I felt her pubic hair brush my lips. I pressed my mouth to her and licked her slowly and nibbled with my lips on her clitoris. She moaned, and grabbed the back of my head pulling me closer. I was hungry for her, for her taste, her smell. About that time Mary took her mouth away and raised herself up and lowered herself on my dick. Oh, the warmth! Different from the mouth, but good! Her vagina gripped me and slid up and down on me, I don't ever remember being as hard as I was at that moment. Her arms came around Sheryl, and were holding her breasts as she rode me. I hoped if I ever died, this is the way I would go.

Then they were moving, Sheryl turned and lifted Mary from me and laid her back and buried her face between Mary's legs. A look of ecstasy came over Mary. And where was I? I was left facing Sheryl's sweet little ass pointed directly at my raging hard on. I eased up behind her and slipped it inside her. She moaned and so did Mary. I gathered I did something right, so I continued. I normally probably would have gotten off by now, maybe, since time had now stood still. I had no idea how long we been there, but I was not going away. This must have gone on for a minute or an hour or four, who knows?

Then Sheryl pulled herself away from me and both girls sit up. They look at each other and giggle then kiss passionately. That was enough to have caused an explosion. They stopped and looked down at my dick, then both pushed me back against the wall of the bunk, both came face to face with each other with my dick between them. They both started licking and sucking me and kissing each other as they did it. They must have worked me over for another month or so, but as I watched the erotic scene in front of me and came to realize it was my dick that was being used for an all day sucker. Suddenly, it started to rise in me. My heart pounded, my body stiffened, and I raised my self off the bunk, and exploded. The greedy little Mary didn't let Sheryl have any of the reward.

It didn't matter. I wasn't done for yet. It must have been three or four in the morning when Mary finally got dressed, hugged us both and kissed us and said goodbye. I will never forget that, my first threesome, with two of the best women that ever made love to a man.

Wow, I need a cigarette now just remembering, and I don't even smoke!

My alarm went off at 6:30; I slipped into my jeans and boots and moved out to the driver's seat to give Sheryl some personal room. The fuel island in front of my truck was full of police cars and sheriff's cars. The area was roped off, including our truck. An ambulance set in front of the truck where all the pushing and shouting had come from the night before. A uniformed officer walked by the front of my truck.

I called out, "Hey, Officer, what's going on?"

"Just sit tight, Driver. Someone will be by to talk to you in a few minutes."

"Ok. Any chance my partner can go to the bathroom? We just got up and nature is calling."

"Hang on just a minute. I will get someone down here."

I turned back and told Sheryl to spray some perfume back there, and make sure there were no signs of drugs showing in case they wanted inside the truck.

In a couple of minutes a plainclothes detective showed up. He stepped up on the running board. I asked him if he would like to come inside and he nodded yes. I slid over into the passenger seat, and he sat in the driver's side.

He looked around, looked at the instrument panel, and said, "Wow, this is really nice. I had no idea. Looks like an airplane from all the dials and gauges. Nice and roomy too. And smells good!"

About that time Sheryl pulled the curtain open and said hello. You could see by the look on his face he was surprised. He glanced back into the sleeper.

"You know, maybe I am in the wrong business," he chuckled.

I smiled. "Detective, what is going on? We need to get moving soon."

He looked back at me. "Your name is....?"

"Oh, sorry. Evan Smith. This is my partner, Sheryl Stevens."

"Well, Mr. Smith, Miss Stevens, did you notice anything out of the ordinary since you have been here?"

"We arrived late yesterday. Just got our new truck delivered to us and picked up our first load. It was a long day so we decided to spend the night here before we left. Yes, just after we arrived, maybe nine or so, there were two guys pushing each other around and shouting a lot. Then one left. A little later, there was more shouting. We went to bed shortly after that. What happened?"

The detective asked me to describe the two guys. I did.

"Evan, the guy in the brown shirt you described was found this morning, hanging on a meat hook. Someone had rammed it into the back of his neck and hung him up."

"Oh shit!"

My thoughts raced back to past evening. In this closed in world in which we lived, a wonder that two things so far apart could happen so close to each other. I shuddered.

"Have you found out who did it?"

"Well, kind of. We have his description, in fact the other guy you mentioned. We know he was driving a white Freightliner cab-over, pulling a flatbed. Don't know what the company was. Witnesses' saw him pull out about midnight, don't know which way. Keep your eyes open since you actually saw him."

"Any idea why he did it?"

"Yeah, it was over a commercial girl. Evidently the guy on the meat hook got really rough with her. Bad enough till the other guys saw him hit her, she had to go to the hospital, beat up pretty bad. I shouldn't say this, but the guy probably got what he deserved. Anyway, you two are free to go whenever your ready. Thanks for the patience."

When he left we turned and looked at each other. Then Sheryl said, "I gotta go to the bathroom." We grabbed our shower bags and a change of underwear, and booked it inside.

After a quick shower and breakfast, it was time to put the Pete into the wind.

After the Banning scales, it was east bound on I-10 for the remainder of the trip, with the exception of a small jaunt at Buckeye, Arizona down to Gila Bend and short stretch of I-8 to Eloy, then back on I-10 again.

We climbed Indio Hill quite easily, not working the big Cat too hard. I glanced to the north at the range of mountains bordering the San Andreas Fault line, and realized, for the first time, that they didn't go straight up. They kinda leaned towards the fault to the west. Up and over the top, across the desert, the heat shimmered in the distance, making you think of waves along the seashore.

Later that evening we stopped at a little truck stop in Van Horn, Texas. We had dinner and went back to the truck. As Sheryl was shedding clothes to head for the sleeper, I looked back behind the truck stop and saw a white Freightliner cab-over. It was the driver from the Ontario Truck Stop! I called to Sheryl, "Hey, Sheryl! There is the guy that probably killed that guy last night! Should I call the law?"

She came up and looked out.

"I never saw him really well last night. It is up to you, but if he was the one that did it and he did it cause that guy fucked up that girl, I couldn't be mad at him. And do we really know he was the one? If that guy was that kinda person, he might have had many people that were pissed at him. I would stay out of it, myself."

I looked at her. That was sound reasoning. I liked her thinking. I had known a guy in 'Nam that shot a fellow soldier cause he had openly raped a girl and beat her up. I had let that go, cause I kinda agreed with it.

"You know what, partner? You are a damned good driver, and a great partner, but you have a good head. I like your thinking. Oh, you're kinda cute too."

All I got for that was a smile and a middle finger.

"Kinda cute, hmmm?" she replied.

I fired the Cat and we eased back out onto I-10, mindful of our delivery time in Houston the next day. Soon, the entire way from El Paso to Houston would be complete. What a drive that would be then. But for tonight, there would be those patches that were and those that weren't.

When we got rolling eastbound, Sheryl slid into the passenger seat, in all her naked glory. She took a hit on the joint she had just rolled, and held it for me. I took it and puffed it one time, and handed it back.

"Evan, about last night. That was really fun, and I enjoyed it a lot, but that won't happen every time. I don't want you to be disappointed when it doesn't."

"Sheryl, I am not quite that fragile. Don't you worry about it. I would not want it to happen every time, or even that often. Now, it was great, don't get me wrong, but, I really am the kind of person that prefers a one on one type of thing. The coke made it what it was. I will always remember it as one of the outstanding experiences of my life. Oh, by the way, I really don't want to get into the coke thing either. It was fun, but I don't feel like I am myself on it or speed."

She looked at me and smiled a bit.

"I am with you Driver, all the way. You know, we think so much alike."

With that she disappeared into the sleeper, not to return until we pulled into our yard later the next morning.

Michelle met me as I got the truck stopped and shut down.

"Nice truck, Evan! It's really pretty!"

"Thanks, Michelle. It's nice and it does the job."

"Well, it's a good thing, cause you got a hot one. Get out from under that trailer and get under the lowboy. I will have the local driver take it on to Houston."

"We have a local driver?"

She laughed, "Yeah, it became a necessity. He only works part time. He is an older fellow, retired, needs something to do. You will meet him in a few minutes. We have a piece of equipment that is in a hurry to get to Spokane, Washington from Dallas. They are waiting for you."

Sheryl was already in the driver's seat.
"I'll get it Evan. Go do your thing.

We went inside. Michelle remarked, "That girl is a real go getter, isn't she?"

"Michelle, she is worth far more than I could ever pay her!"

I picked up my permits for the new truck, and did some paperwork. By that time Sheryl had come in with a man in his early to mid 60's. He had a cowboy-ish look to him, his face was carved out of saddle leather. Thin but not skinny.

"Evan, meet Hank. He helped me get the lowboy hooked up. We are ready to roll anytime. Hank, this is Evan, the best boss a driver could have!"

I shook hands.

"Good to meet you, Hank. Sheryl is great at instilling fear of management at our little company. I guess you are worried sick about pleasing me now."

"Tony and Michelle had just about took the bite outta ya, anyhow. Sheryl just kinda put the icing on ya, but I ain't real apt to try to raise the ire in a man anyhow. Pleased to make yur 'quaintance. I'll try to do ya a fair job."

"I'm sure you will Hank. But will you call me, when they put the night club with the dancing girls and the pool in?"

"I'll do that, Boss."

"No Boss. Just Evan will do. And I am sorry to

greet and run, but these people here don't want me to stay around here much. Somehow, probably think I'll get in their way."

With that we left. We hit I-35 up to Dallas. By dark we were loaded and tied down, and got our bills straight. We went east a ways and found US 287 and headed toward Amarillo. I had taken a quick shower at the yard, and so had Sheryl. We found a mom and pop restaurant that we could get into and had a good dinner. They had a good salad bar that really hit the spot. An hour later I was in dreamland and Sheryl was chasing white lines toward the panhandle.

Life was like that for the next few years. We worked together becoming perfect teammates. We seldom, if ever, quarreled. If one of us was having a bad day, the other one just stayed out of the way. We put over a half million miles on the Pete by 1980. We grew as a company. Things changed, as they always do in business. We had two more teams with us now making a total of four. Hank, our local guy, finally retired after 4 more years, and we hired another local guy. This one worked pretty much full time. Houston started booming in 1980 and 1981, we were getting more and more work out of there.

When an area starts to grow, it requires materials and goods, and most of it is trucked in, creating jobs and truck traffic. We had trouble sometimes getting loads out of Houston, but there was lots coming in.

I ran into Larry Murley again one morning in July in Houston. He was driving for a company that hauled a lot of government stuff based in Joplin, Missouri. They had a terminal on I-45 North. He had him a new girl, and this time she was driving with him. Her name was Connie. Cute little blonde girl in her early 20's, Larry was now in his early 40's. They made a nice couple.

We went and had dinner with them, and visited a couple of hours. The two of us talked about trucks and Vietnam, and the girls chatted about, well, whatever girls chat about. I told him about my writing the trucking stories down, and that I had included his. He asked if I had been east very much. I told him that I had. He told me that he had just come down from Jersey and had been at Rubes Truck Stop in Jersey City. He said he had left Connie in the truck with the doors locked with instructions to not unlock them for anyone. While he was inside the building, a guy came running, cursing everything in sight. Said he had backed his truck up in the corner and went to sleep the evening before. He had just awoke and got out to find that his truck was up on blocks and all 10 wheels and tires were gone. He had slept through the whole thing! He told the manager to call the cops. The manager told him to "Forgetaboutit! Goddamn cops ain't gonna help ya, go buy ya some new tires. And get your ass outta my truck stop, ya stupid prick. You must be a real dead ass!"

Larry said he couldn't help thinking the manager knew more about it than he was saying. I thanked him and said I would add that one to the story as well. They were loading for somewhere else, and we were as well, so we said our goodbyes.

It never ceases to amaze me how life directs you. The decisions you make today may shape your life forever. The people you meet that influence your life in as many different ways as there are people. I wondered at Larry. When I first met him, he was a solid, hardworking guy with a family, two kids. He seemed to always score good jobs, yet there was something about him that seemed sad, or missing. A restlessness. He didn't talk much about Vietnam, but I knew from talking to him there must be the same ghosts present that haunted the rest of us. I wondered if he would ever tell me any more. He always seemed to change the subject when it got serious.

It had been 12 or 13 years now since I had gotten back from Southeast Asia. I was in my mid thirties now. My mind was now full of my business. I have great people around me that work with me, I have a successful life. But now, all of a sudden, the dreams came back, and I found myself waking in a cold sweat, sometimes crying, without much memory of what I am dreaming. Other times, it was like a technicolor movie - men shouting, the smell of burning things, helicopters blades chopping the air, weapons firing, fireballs in the jungle. And I saw enemy soldiers coming at me, and I would try to raise my weapon and fire at them, but either I couldn't raise it up, or it wouldn't fire, or if it did, the bullets just roll out of the end of the barrel. I would pick them up and put them back in, but when I tried to level the weapon, they would roll back out again, and the enemy kept coming closer.

Then, Sheryl would shake me awake.

"Evan, you alright?"

We talked about it. I didn't understand why, now, they are coming back. We discussed it, and then one afternoon Sheryl said, "Evan, maybe earlier you were working so hard, your subconscious didn't have time to dwell on this. Maybe now, ... maybe now that you have a life, suddenly there is a fear that you can't defend it, or it's to big to protect. And that is connecting you to that terrible time in your life."

"Then what's the answer? How do I get this out of me, and rid myself of these memories?"

She was silent. She continued to drive for a while. I could tell she was deep in thought, she looked so serious. We had gotten to know each other so well over the years. She was indispensable in my life now. Our affection was almost unspoken, but as real as a couple could be if they had been married for half their lives.

"Evan, maybe the answer is not to try to rid your self of those memories, or to try to bury them. Maybe the answer is to bring them out of the dark, out into the light, where they can be seen and examined and understood. We have been together for seven years now. I know you were in Vietnam. I have seen your scars, yet, I have no idea what you experienced, or what you saw. I watched TV and saw the combat footage, but I, like most everyone else, have no idea what it was like."

"It's hard to talk about Sheryl. Much of it you are scared to death, or you are doing things that you are later ashamed of. It is not an easy subject."

"Still, would you tell me your story? From the first day you were there, till the last day you left. Tell me everything, don't leave out anything. I want to know every aspect of your life during that time."

"I will have to think about it, I will let you know. There are some things I don't know if I can put words to."

And I did. I thought about it. I realized that psychiatrists do about the same thing with their patients. They get them to talk about their thoughts. But then there were those episodes that you know you had no choice with, that the world would consider immoral, or maybe even illegal. War causes situations that most people never have to face. Survival creates decisions, born out desperation, otherwise unimaginable.

Finally one morning, I made my decision.

We had just rolled out of Kansas City Westbound, headed for the Shaky side again. Sheryl had just started driving, nothing much to see for the next 600 miles or so. I pulled a joint out of the ash tray and lit it and took a hit, then another, and passed it to her. She puffed and passed it back.

"Sheryl, my good friend, are you ready to hear about Vietnam?"

She turned her head, and looked at me.

"If you are ready to tell me!"

"Well, being ready is not the issue. I am not sure I could ever ready myself. Some of the things may make you want to judge me. I hope not, but you have asked me, and I see merit in it's possibilities. So, here goes...."

For the next eight hours I told her everything I could remember. I told her of the oppressive heat, the insects and the snakes, the grass as tall as your head, and of the filth of living and sweating and shitting, and not being able to wash and clean yourself thoroughly. Of night patrols, and silent patrols in the jungle. I told her of the VC habits. Of herding women and children in front of them for living shields, sometimes booby trapping them with explosives. Of sometimes being forced to kill innocent civilians to save your self and your comrade's lives.

I talked about the dangers of walking point, of ambushes and being surrounded by large forces. Of helicopter drops in hot LZ's, and the sometimes drudgery of the daily life. I remembered the rains, of sitting in the rain so intense that it seemed to come up under the ponchos as well as down on them. Of being wet to the core, but never clean. I talked about being afraid, but still moving forward. I talked about the camaraderie of your brothers in arms, of how you put aside the necessity of understanding the war, and all the things it encompasses, and just living for your buddies, making sure they were okay. I talked about the people. The men and women whose war it was, from a little child to a grown adult, not a year out of their life, or two. They were born in it, and too many of them died in it. About the country itself. It had been once beautiful, exotic, some parts probably a paradise. But now a country defoliated, bombed, shelled, burned by Napalm. The roads rutted by war equipment.

The more I talked and cried, I could see tears rolling down her cheeks as she sailed her mighty ship into the west. I couldn't remember ever having cried about Vietnam. It was like leaving a theater after watching a really powerful and soul touching movie. It left you impacted, but you didn't know how to react. So you just didn't.

When I finally stopped the tale, I explained about how trucking had become the bandage on my wounds, and the key to my prison.

Somehow, for the first time in years, I felt a bit lighter. More like a huge secret had been exposed, and no one had blamed me for it.

Sheryl sighed. She dropped her rpm, and her right turn signal came on. I noticed she was pulling into a rest area. She pulled into a parking place and set the brake. The sun was low in the western sky, casting golden beams through the windshield, lighting the back wall of the sleeper.

She motioned. "Go back there." I did and laid back on the bunk. She followed me back and lay down, putting her arms around me and her face into my neck. I could feel her tears. She lay very close for a long time. I held her in my arms. It is only fitting that after War, one should find a place of peace. That afternoon it was somewhere along the Kansas-Colorado border on the side of the Interstate in a rest area.

After maybe a half hour, she raised her head and kissed me, very softly.

"Evan, thank you for sharing that. I won't dishonor it by saying I'm sorry or pitying you. It was your journey and it was what it was. You did what you had to do. I have two Uncles now that I understand more because of this. As you remember other incidents, tell them to me as well. Open all the windows of your mind and let the sunlight in. I watched the last rays of the sun disappear somewhere ahead behind the mighty Rockies."

We hit Denver about 10 pm and passed on through and up and over the front range, climbing high towards Loveland Pass and the Continental Divide. We passed through the Eisenhower Tunnel and geared down for the seven miles of 7% grade down to Dillon. We were about two miles down the hill when the radio came on, everyone trying to talk at once.

"Lookout below! Runaway truck! Runaway truck! He is moving fast, real fast! Outta control!"

I glanced back in my mirrors. I could see a pair of headlights coming up really fast. He blew by us like we were up on jacks, must have been doing a hundred miles an hour. I kept myself as slow as I could, even dropped another gear so as to not heat my brakes. This was not going to end well, I thought. Way ahead, I saw a flash, and then darkness.

I eased on down. There were two or three trucks stopped with flashers going by the time I arrived. I set my four ways and my brakes, and got out and put a couple of chock blocks in front of the drive wheels.

I walked down to the debris pile. People were clawing their way into the remains of a large sedan, maybe a Lincoln or Cadillac. The driver had run over it, literally. There was another car up on the right hand bank pretty much destroyed as well. He had hit it and sent it flying, before he ran over the other car.

When we got into the big car, there were two bodies, both old people. They were headless and mutilated, arms separated from their bodies. They never saw him coming. Likely they were driving out in the passing lane.

Somebody said, "There are four in the car up on the bank! Looks like a family. At least two dead, others are in a bad way."

By then we could see the red lights and hear the sirens coming from both directions.

I was a bit worried another truck would come down too fast, but someone had said on the CB that they were stopping them at the tunnel before they started down. It was about that time someone yelled, "There's another car up here under the tractor!" We ran around the other side. The cab of the tractor was just gone, couldn't even tell what it was. I asked about the driver. Some one said he was dead over in the ditch in the median.

We found another vehicle up under the frame,

sideways. You could tell the rig had been sliding it sideways down the road after it crashed. We tore parts off, trying to get into it. I looked down. My hands were bleeding. Finally, we could get to the door. The door was yanked or torn open.

Inside was a young woman, probably early 30's. She was bloody and cut, and her right arm was lying at an angle. Her left leg was broken as well. She opened her eyes and said, "My baby! Please, save my baby!" I leaned over her and looked. In the other floorboard on the passenger side, I could see a little boy, about three or four. He looked fine, just as though he had fallen asleep. I felt his leg, there was a pulse.

I turned around and said, "He is alive! I can't see his injuries, he is unconscious."

The lady was pinned, the steering wheel was across her abdomen and something else had her right foot pinned.

Sheryl was standing beside me, a look of horror on her face. I turned to her.

"Sheryl, I am going to hold on to your hips and

216

support you, lean across her very carefully, see if you can get under the baby with your arms, kind of making a backboard with your forearms, and lift him and I will pull you out."

She did, I could see her under him, and I slowly lifted her back past the mothers face. The boy whimpered a bit. The mother was crying. As we got him out, two or three ambulances were arriving, and more bears.

Sheryl held him. I felt carefully around him. He was not bleeding, and I couldn't find any broken bones, but he had a nasty bump on his head. One of the paramedics came running up, and then another. The second had a gurney, and we placed the little boy on the gurney and left him in the capable hands of the paramedics. Firemen started working to free the mother - basically, ripping the car apart until finally they were able to lift her onto another gurney.

As we walked back to the truck, I stopped at a CHP officer and handed him my card. I told him if he needed any information to call he said he would. He glanced down at my hands and said, "You Okay?" I said I was. He told me to go over to the ambulance and have one of the guys wash and disinfect my hands at least.

I nodded ok, and we walked over and got some band-aids where needed.

Back in the truck, I turned to Sheryl.

"I have seen a lot of wrecks, but that was a bad one!"

She nodded.

We hit the bottom of the hill took the first exit and pulled across in front of a convenience store. I bought me a Dr. Pepper, and we were westbound again.

We climbed out and up over Vail Pass, down across the flatlands through Eagle, and into Glenwood Canyon, winding along through the curves along side the mighty Colorado River. It was a moonlit night, and the cliffs were lit by the sparkling river below. Too soon we were out and through Glenwood Springs, and sped across more levels. Through Rifle and back along the Colorado, and down through Palisades into Grand Junction.

We climbed the Red Mountain pass into Utah, headed for a connection with I-15 out somewhere ahead.

Somewhere out in the desert wastes of Utah we changed drivers. I was thinking about the bedroom behind me. After last night I was pretty tired. As Sheryl was busy going through the shifting pattern, a couple of Monforts blew by us.

"Hey, Black Pete! You got your communicator on?"

"Yes Sir. Go ahead."

"Just wanted you to know, the lady and the little boy made it. I remembered you were there with them."

"Great! Thanks very much, I really appreciate that."

"No Problem. See ya down the road a ways."

By that time Sheryl had found high gear and we were rolling along at about the same speed. One of the drivers said to the other, "Hey Swangin', did I ever tell you about that time Smokey told me about that runaway over on Rabbit Ears Pass?"

"No Sir. You never did. Go ahead."

"Roger Beep on that. Well, here goes. Hang on to your steering wheel. He said way back in the 70's when they was putting a 'automatic truck stopping ramps' on Rabbit Ears, they was just about done with it. The two highway trucks were setting at the approach to the ramp about 8 feet apart, facing the ramp, and the dozer driver was spreading the gravel up the ramp almost to the top. Anyway, this old boy from the flatlands came flying over the top, and you how Rabbit Ears is. It don't look bad for about a mile. Well, he realized that, but at his speed he used his breaks up in nothing flat, and here he went! He said by the time he got to the last curve above the ramp, he looked down and his speedo was pegged." Here the driver chuckled slightly. "He saw the two trucks, but decided he had to try to go between them, so that's where he headed. He hit his air horn just as he arrived. He went between those to state trucks, and up the ramp! Somewhere near the top, the dozier driver looks back and sees this KW just about to catch him! He bales off the dozier, falls down the mountainside, breaks his arm." Here he is openly snickering. "The dozer just keeps on going, up over the top and falls into a canyon on the other side, doing it no good. The KW comes to a stop just in time. The driver was okay, 'cept he needed some new drawers. But the two state guys had to go to the hospital, it scared them so bad! All they heard was a horn and the flash of an 18 wheeler, inches away from them! This CHP officer that told me this, he laughed till he cried telling me this story!"

"Dammit, Road Ranger! I have set here and laughed till I almost pee'd my pants! Funniest thing I ever heard!"

"But that is a dangerous hill though. There have been some not so lucky. The way it is exposed, snow will melt, then refreeze. It just gets greasier than shit."

"10-4 on that. It sure does."

I keyed the mike. "Ranger, thanks for sharing. That is another story for my book of truck stories."

"Roger that. Who we got back there?"

"They call me Wind Walker. And Shadow is doing

the steering at the moment."

"10 Roger. The other dude is Swingin' Meat - or least he says so. And I am the world famous Road Ranger, at your service! We got your front door, Shadow!"

We ran with the two guys most all day, then stopped at Barstow to catch the morning rush past the Cajon scales halfway down the grade.

The deal was, we would wait for a huge run of trucks heading in-bound. Then, as they piled up at the scales, they would turn the open light off and let everyone bypass the port of entry.

Much easier that way. We made our 3 am delivery on time. We had left New Jersey on Friday evening about 7:30 pm. Coast to coast over the weekend!

I couldn't help thinking of Cat when we went to the Shaky side. I had called her terminal several times in the past, but she wasn't ever there when I called. Finally, I got the "Dear Evan" letter. She had met someone else, she would always care for me, and was sorry we didn't work out, but sometimes that is the way things happen. I had certainly cared for her as well, but we just seemed to go in different directions. But I would always have fond memories of her.

Next morning, we were dispatched up to Santa Clara for a load of produce going to Portland. I started to turn it down since it was such a short haul. I called Michelle and she said take it, she had a load waiting up there going all the way to the east coast. So we did it and next morning off loaded in downtown Portland. I asked Sheryl if she had ever been to the Jubitz. She said no, she hadn't been northwest very much. I told her she was going to get a treat.

Michelle had us scheduled for a lease lowboy pickup the next morning and a loading time late afternoon at Boeing in Seattle. So we cruised up to the north side of Portland and pulled into the parking lot. Sheryl said, "This looks nice."

"Sheryl, grab your bags. We are going to spend the night in a real room tonight!"

We went inside, registered for a room, dropped our clothes, went to the restaurant, and had a late lunch. Out in the lobby, I took her by the hand and led her inside the honky-tonk doors.

"OH MY! Evan, this IS different!"

"Yep. And wait until tonight!"

We went back up and crashed for a two or three hours. We had been running pretty hard for several weeks, and it felt good to stretch out in a bed that didn't move.

When we woke up, it was dark outside. I got up and stepped into the shower. I let the hot water warm my whole body. I couldn't but help remember my first time here with Cat.

I stepped out and as I did Sheryl called out, "Leave the water running!"

I toweled off as she brushed by me and stepped in the running water. I trimmed my beard and shaved my neck. I was dressed when she stepped out. My date for the evening was ever bit as fine as my date for the first evening at the Jubitz had been. I told her I would wait for her in the restaurant, to take her time.

She just smiled.

I went out to the restaurant. I sat in a booth near the window. Two drivers were talking about the eruption of Mount St. Helens the year before.

The first said "I will never forget it. I was coming down 5 from Seattle. I looked off to my left, and there was this huge pillar of smoke. I thought to my self, 'That is a huge fire!' Then I hit an open spot, and I could see it was the top of a mountain! I thought 'Oh my God! It's a volcano eruption!' I never expected to see one."

The other guy nodded, and answered with, "Yeah, I live up in Chehalis. We have a pool at our apartment. When we heard the damn thing go off, I went outside and was standing on the deck and I looked down and you could see a big crack come in the bottom of the pool, and the water just started draining out. It was a horrible time. People were saying they're all gonna erupt, all the way up the chain. Hood and Rainier, and they erupt and the west coast is done for. Like Armageddon, you know, but it didn't."

"Nope just goes to show you nature don't always pay attention to what people say."

I thought about that. My time back in 1970 when I camped out in Yellowstone. I think I realized then that humans were just a spec in comparison to the planet. Still, we do a lot of damage to the planet, with the mining and the pollution. Almost any big city has a big brown cloud over it. I was still thinking about it when Sheryl slid into the booth beside me.

Wow, she cleaned up really good! First time I had ever seen her in a dress and heels. She was wearing a burgundy sweater and a black skirt and red heels. Her long black hair was down and swept back.

"Damn, girl! You don't look like a truck driver!"

"Right now, I don't really feel like one."

After dinner we wandered into the lounge. It wasn't as crowded as it was the first time with Cat. But then again it wasn't a weekend.

By 10 pm, however, a good crowd had arrived. The band was starting to rock. We had danced a couple of dances. Sheryl was a good dancer, but I really think it's just the nature of girls to be better dancers.

About 11 pm two young ladies came in and took the table next to ours. Both blonde, both very pretty. They had obviously been drinking before they arrived. It wasn't long before a couple of drivers had asked them to dance. One, in particular, seemed to appeal to them. A tall, dark haired guy about 40. He danced with each of them, then would return, and sat between them. They were each kissing him and each other at the same time. It got pretty erotic, the more inebriated they become. We couldn't help watching them. The music was good, it was a real party atmosphere.

Sheryl said, "Damn, Evan, that about turns me on! I could do with them for a while."

The driver across from us evidently heard her.

"Pretty lady, don't waste your time, they are regulars here. Once they make their choice, they won't look at anyone else. They act like they like girls, but they are really into each other. They are sisters, and are only really hot for each other. This guy they have selected is gonna have one hot time later, that's for sure."

Sheryl looked at him.

"How come you know so much about it?"

"I got chosen one time. That's all anyone ever gets. Most of the guys here won't mess with them. They get pretty far out. They take the guy home with them and have their way with him and each other, then kick him out when they sober up!"

Sheryl looked back at the girls and said "Wow!"

Sure 'nuff, a little later they all three get up and leave together.

We stayed till about 1 am, and then went back to our room.

Sheryl cuddled up to me and said, "You know what? Those girls started an itch with all that stuff. Feel like scratching it?"

"I will do my best, ma'am."

It didn't take any urging, I had a very strong

attraction to my partner. And the opportunity didn't happen very often. We made love for a half hour or so, then lay and cuddled, and slept close.

Next morning, as we were having breakfast, the driver with the two girls walked in to the restaurant. As he passed, Sheryl looked up and grinned.

"You survived!"

He looked at her and blushed, beet red. He turned and sat down across from us, still blushing.

"Yeah, I survived. I mean to tell you though, that was an experience of a life time! I never dreamed that it would go as far as it did at any time. When they took me out to their car, I figured they would just say good night. But no! One tossed me the keys and told me they were to drunk to drive. On the way home, they made out with each other all the way home. When we got there, they were already naked. They had already done about everything I had ever figured two girls could do with each other. Boy, was I wrong! We had sex all night till about an hour ago. The younger one said thank you, and called me a cab and said get out. I did. Damn, I don't think I would want to go back, it just got too weird!"

Sheryl and I both laughed with him, and bid him a good day.

We went to the rental yard and swapped out our trailer, and headed over to Boeing. We were guided in to one their hangers and pulled along side a huge box. It was about 50 feet long, a full eight foot wide, and about ten feet tall. Shortly, a huge overhead crane rolled over the top of us. The box was strapped and lifted onto our trailer. After putting dunnage under it, I measured our height. We were 13' 9½", overall length 75' long. I called Michelle, and asked her to check permit laws for all the states we would have to cross. The load was headed to Cape Kennedy, Florida.

She said we were legal even for night running. Even with our trailer stretched we still had about a six foot over hang, which required lights at night. We got our bills, and went back to the trailer rental place. Their mechanic put us on a cluster in the middle and turn signals on each side, and wired them into the trailer. We were ready to go in an hour. We headed out across I-90, much the same I had done on my motorcycle 11 years ago. It is a long way from Seattle to the middle of Florida.

We turned south out on the plains west of Spokane, and headed for the Columbia River at Pasco. Our routing would take us down across Idaho, and into the north end of Utah, and out across I-80, to near Omaha. Then down across Missouri to Saint Louis, then down thru Illinois into Tennessee and across thru Choo Choo, and down I-75 into Georgia, and over to Jacksonville then down I-95 to the Cape. Over 3200 miles of good truckin' fun.

Best of all, we had six days to do it in. We did it in five, and didn't particularly rush.

1981 came and went. 1982 found us with another new black Pete, much like the one before but with less miles. We ran most of the 48 these days. We had four teams counting Sheryl and I, and Jim and Jo. We kept diversifying, and expanding our rights. Tony and Michelle were worth their weight in gold. They could find loads for us, when other drivers would sit for days. Some of the loads were not good payers, but they would get us to loads that were.

My book of stories grew all the time. I kept a close ear on the radio and in truck stops where drivers were talking. Sometimes the stories happened to us as well.

Take that night we had loaded up in Maryland and came down I-81 to where it became I-40 in Tennessee. We were out somewhere west of Nashville and west of the Tennessee River. We had been running with three other drivers, two of them with cab-over company trucks, hauling for a company I won't mention. The other was a wise ass owner operator, trying to make time with any girl that came on the radio. You know the type.

Anyway, it came up this really nasty thunderstorm. It was raining, wind was a blowing, lightning striking just constant. It was really nasty. We were out front about a mile. Next was a dude, who called himself Gigolo, in the front cab-over. The owner operator was in the rocking chair, then the other cab-over was a girl who called herself Stargazer.

Well, all a sudden a big bolt of lightning struck really close. It just popped! Gigolo said, "Stargazer, that is just too close for comfort tonight!"

"You got that right, Gigolo. I hate that shit,

'specially with these loads of globynites!"

"10-Roger that, Gigolo! Electricity and globynites aren't good at all."

The little cowboy piped in, "What are y'all talkin' about, globynites?"

Stargazer came back with "Oh, it's what we are haulin' in our little wagons!"

Gigolo said, "Cowboy, Stargazer and I each have about 45,000 lbs of drums of gunpowder in our wagons. It is really scary. Lightning can set it off, or friction from like a panic stop, or a wreck. It's pretty volatile."

About that time there was another really close lightning strike.

Cowboy hollered, "90,000 lbs of gunpowder? Oh shit! I will see you later!"

He was still blowing black smoke when he passed us a few minutes later. Stargazer piped up.

"Yeah! ya see, Cowboy, if one of those lightning

233

strikes hits, it will be just a big glow in the night!"

Sheryl and I laughed the rest of the night about the fraidy-cat cowboy!

It brings up a point though. The public, most of the time, has no idea what is coming at him or her as they drive the highways of America, or probably the world. Trucks haul everything from your food and clothing, your fuel, and everything you use on a daily basis. They also haul construction products, dangerous chemicals, explosives, government munitions, weaponry. You name it and a truck hauls it. You probably never think what would happen with a 8,500 gallon tanker of gasoline would do if it overturned coming at you. Much closer than a hundred feet, and you would probably never survive the fireball. There is an acid called oleum, that if you dropped a drop on the back of your hand, it would instantly burn a hole right through your hand and fall out the bottom. Imagine what 6,000 to 8,000 gallons of that would do to you. They would never find you. That is some of the rare stuff, but there are much more common ones like sulfuric and nitric acids and caustic soda. Of these, vast amounts are used, and on the road every hour of every day. And all manner of explosives, from military grade C-4 to dynamite, gunpowder, ammunition, and various other accelerants used in demolition work. Then we have the fuels - gasoline, diesel fuel, jet-50. For the fighter jets there is JP4. It is so volatile you can dip your fingers in it on a hot day, and flick it off of your fingers and ignite it. Also, the naphtha sand, and many others to numerous to mention. Yeah let's not forget the boys hauling crude out of the oil fields. It burns too, you know. Okay, now those are the dangerous items.

Now, how about the loads of pipe, lumber, raw materials of any kind, almost anything you can put on an open trailer. It all must be safely tied down. Now, there are many, many, many, responsible, well trained truck drivers out there who tie their loads down securely and safely. But unfortunately, we all have Mortimer Snerd and Joe Blow that don't have brains enough to come in out of the rain. Yeah, they sometimes get commercial licenses too. And even if they get training, there are those who will always be lazy or negligent. And it only takes one time - a sharp corner, a panic stop - and 45,000 lbs of cargo is tumbling off onto some bodies Ford Station Wagon full of kids.

I hope I made my point. Be aware. Keep your eyes

on that 80,000 lb behemoth coming at you at 70 mph. Don't take it for granted. Ok, let's get back to the fun stuff now.

Once, on a trip up to the northwest, we had just passed through the little town of La Grande, Oregon. It had been snowing a bit, but not cold enough to be frozen. About four or five big trucks were all running together. Sunday traffic, we were just approaching the canyon, heading up into the Blues, when the lead driver, yells back, "Hey! Watch out! It's greasy up here!"

Everyone started backing out of it, except the four wheelers. They didn't know. About that time, this four wheeler passed me, pulling a trailer with a snowmobile on it. He had no sooner got around me, when he went into a fishtail. Ever time he turned, that snowmobile would slap him on the side then go back around to the other side and slap him again. Back and forth, while he was spinning round and round going down the middle of the road. I started to try to brake, but whenever I tried my trailer would try to come around so I would let up. I managed to stay behind him until we were into the first curve to the right. He was stopping, but I couldn't. I was really slow now but still sliding.

Finally, I watched him disappear under the front of the big black Hood. Then I stopped. It was then that I saw this hand and arm come up into view, just waving at me. I laughed. And then, my whole rig, in a straight line, just slid over to the guardrail on the low side, and stopped. In about a mile stretch, about 12 four wheelers and four big trucks came to a rest. No one hurt, no real damage. It could have been a disaster.

As we cruised the country, we watch life's dramas unfold around us. We saw people living in big trucks, most of the time in a hurry, deadlines to meet. In the trucking life, access to anything other than the highway and truck stops and an occasional rest area is extremely limited.

But I would see people try to bring their pets with them. I suppose cats are feasible, although I have sat in trucks that had cats residing in them. I never liked that odor, and although cat lovers will tell you that it was just an irresponsible cat owner that didn't change their litter box, they all smelled that way.

Then there were the ones that would have a full

sized dog with them. Folks, that is just damned inhumane. That dog is never going to get the exercise he needs. He is going to have to spend extended periods of time in a cramped space. Not good. A small breed would maybe be a better idea.

I have a thing about seeing dogs on chains. I knew a guy in Vietnam that had been chained, before some Special Forces guys found him and rescued him. He was always just a lit fuse, trying to find an explosive. And you didn't want to touch him for no reason. I think maybe that is why most chained dogs become vicious. I bought many a burger in truck stops and take them outside and fed some poor stray that was starving to death. I never understood people abandoning dogs. We saw so many along side the highways that had been run over and killed. I guess by then I had seen enough killing and pain. I just didn't want to see any more. Sheryl wasn't a real animal person, she said she wasn't brought up around animals and just never developed a fondness for them. I suppose that worked out real good for our life style.

One night we had delivered out on Long Island and were headed back out to Jersey to get another load when this voice came over the radio.

238

"Anyone out there got an extra $20?"

I grinned. I picked up the mic and said, "What do want the 20 for dear?"

She answered, "Well, we ate dinner a while ago, out on the Island and we are headed back to Jersey now. We have a com-check waiting, but we run outta cash and these assholes on the outbound Throg's Neck Bridge won't let us out!"

I laughed. The Throg's Neck isn't toll on the way in, but it is on the way out.

I hollered back, "Where you at?"

"We are just past the gate on the side, the back of our trailer says TSMT."

As I approached the toll booth I could see sitting just past it a dry box with TSMT at the top. I paid my toll and fished an extra $20 out of my wallet. As I did, I pointed at the TSMT trailer and asked the toll guy would $20 cover those drivers? He nodded yes. I pulled up beside the other truck. My passenger door opened and a tall pretty blonde was standing there.

I handed her the $20. She said, "We will pay you back soon as we get our com-check. Are you going to the truck stop?"

I smiled and said, "This one is on me. Be sure and shut my door good, I gotta go!"

I looked back and watched her watch me drive away. I would probably never see her again. But you know what? It was kinda like helping family. We all were kind of an extended family.

The East Coast was always a difficult place. It's streets are narrow, especially for the big rigs that were becoming so commonplace. Some places we would go to deliver were made for horses and wagons or single axle trucks. The freeways many of them were divided by miles of concrete dividers, like concrete canyons. The driver had to pay close attention, or he would be scrubbing one side or the other. Then there was the roughness. I could write a book about the roughness. Both I-80 and the Pennsylvania Pike would sometimes have whole sections where the re-bar would be exposed. Bad for tires, and bad for co-drivers trying to sleep on those roads.

Then there were the speed limits. Ever since Mr. Nixon had instituted the 55 mph speed limit in '74, we had all had to deal with that. Some states were more lenient than others. Two of the worst were Ohio and Connecticut. They would write you for two miles over. They seemed like they spent their entire budgets paying for Smokeys to sit in the medians. And they weren't nice Smokeys either. Some of them were real storm troopers.

So it was always a real treat to get back out west. It always seemed that north and south traffic was always so much more relaxed than east and west, for some reason or the other.

One of those up and down trips was a good example of that. It was a beautiful spring morning and we were coming up from the Sunshine State. We had picked up a load just outside Little Cuba and we were headed for Boston.

I had got started talking with another driver going the same way on I-95. We were being real bucket mouths, deep in some philosophical discussion. At one point, a voice broke in on our conversation.

"Drivers, I hate to interrupt such a good bit of gab, but you just run our Port of Entry for the great Commonwealth of Virginia, and we just can't have that. About two or so miles up the road is an overpass. Make a turnaround there and comeback past us. About 3 miles past us, there is another turn around. Take it and let's try to hit the entrance to the Port this time. Oh, yeah, bring in all your logs, bills, and paperwork. See you shortly, gentlemen!"

"Yes Sir!"

"Yes Sir!"

About 15 minutes later we were pulling across the scales. We took our paper work inside, looking very sheepish. We were met with loud laughter and a bit of chiding, but it was all very good natured. They checked our papers, which all happened to be in order for both of us. The scale man said they had been listening to us on their base station for some time before we got there, and they just about crapped there pants when we just zoomed right by. They were still laughing when we walked out the door.

I never, ever, missed another port after that.

That must have been sometime in '86, cause it was the last time I remember seeing Larry. He was driving for a Colorado meat hauler. We had stopped at the big truck stop on I-80, just before you get to Jersey. He was now with wife number three. He and I talked about our lives, and how they had changed. He seemed to like trucking, said if he got down to Austin he would come see me. I went west and he went east, never more to meet.

Like all jobs, driving has it's up's and downs.

There are the days with sunny dry roads and beautiful scenery. There are the nights, wet roads, blowing snow, and narrow pavement. Sometimes you have a tailwind, and trip is over before you realize it. Then there was the one pulling this huge hunk of fabricated steel. I was headed for Portland with it. All the way across I-80 from Laramie to Utah. The wind was blowing about 50 mph and gusting right out of the west-northwest. I couldn't pull it over about 45 or 50 most of the time. Those are the times that make you want to smoke a lot of weed, and I probably did. This was back before I had a co-driver, or even a radio. That makes for some kind of record boredom. I spent my time fantasizing about the early pioneers and mountain men crossing there in the mid 1800's. It may have made me feel better, I don't know.

The advent of the CB radio was a great help in easing the boredom for the single driver. Now there seemed to always be someone to talk to, and sometime to listen to.

Many times I have listened to a driver coming at me somewhere down the road, singing. Sometimes excellent singers with awesome voices. Many times I wished we were going the same way. And then there were the story tellers. I remember one that was telling this story. As usual he was going the wrong way. I found myself slowing down, slower and slower, hoping he would finish before he got out of radio range. Finally, he finished. Seconds later, this voice came over the radio.

"Goddamn, man! I pulled over on the shoulder and waited for a minute. I thought I was gonna have to turn around in the median and chase him down to hear the rest. Dammit, I hate guys like that!"

Another driver came back, "Yessir, I had my eye

on a turnaround point, but I just made it!"

Strange but interesting things that move by you like film on a projector, huge frames, that make you wonder, "What on Earth is that for?"

Then there was big pipe we picked up in Wilmington, North Carolina. It was 60' feet long, smaller at one end and straight and getting larger to the other end, belling out and making a 90% bend a the big end. It was going to some kind of plant south of Shreveport, Louisiana.

For two days it was statements like, "Driver, that is the biggest pot pipe I ever saw!" or "Driver, do you have another truck some where with a load of weed to fill that thing?" or "Driver, that's gonna take a lotta suckin' to get a hit through that!"

"Hey, Driver! I gotta connection on a guy that's got five acres of weed you could partner up with!"

"Hey, Driver! where's the party tonight?"

"Driver, my old lady could suck that thing red hot in a minute!"

I was so glad to get rid of that thing. Late in the day I just turned my radio off.

Then there was the poor Coca Cola drivers one morning coming out of Denver going southbound. Coca Cola has a white swirly line that runs down the length of the trailer. Obviously, it is just too much for some drivers with weird sense of humors. The first one passed, and as he did you heard this sucking sound, like someone sucking something up their nose come over the radio. Then, "Wow, man, that was good shit!" followed by "Hey, Coke, you got any extra straws?"

"Hey, Coke, is that the 'Real Thing'?"

And that went on for a while.

Then sometimes around the truck stops, especially near a city, someone with a big powerful station, usually a base station, will just throw a silent carrier by keying the mic and just holding it, or play music or something obnoxious, like a preacher preaching, or some wild rant. All you can do then is just hit the off button and turn up the tunes.

They can be of so much help, too. My friend Larry, that I have spoken of, told me he was up on a mountain once hauling propane. He got on some ice in the middle of a snow storm and his trailer started to slide. He got stopped, but he only got help when he got hold of a base station who called his company and sent some equipment to get him back on the road.

Sometime people bought and sold personal items if they needed a little cash. I bought several CB's themselves from drivers in truck stops. I also bought load locks, tarps, tires and other trucking items while on the radio somewhere. In the 80's it reached a point till you could buy anything on a CB radio, from companionship to all kinds of drugs. I pretty much stayed clear of things of this sort. I always kept in mind what I could lose to falling victim to something like this.

There were so many of the lot lizards anymore in truck stops, in roadside rest areas, and in commercial areas where lots of trucks loaded and unloaded. Places like Hunt's Point and Spanish Harlem in the Big Apple. It was a subsidized business, one would think.

I had many opportunities to sample these young ladies, and many of them were quite attractive, but I never believed in paying for sex. I didn't really think it should be outlawed, it is the oldest profession, I am told. But I always thought it should be on a more personal level for me.

One cold, lonely night on the south side of Chicago it was about 2 am, I had pulled in to the truck stop to just get out of the constant snow. Row after row of snow covered 18 wheelers sat idling in the storm, sitting still, with windows up and lights out. They reminded me of silent soldiers, quietly sleeping, waiting to spring forth into action at the first command. But now resting until the next day's battle. I took a hit on a joint and settled back in my seat for a few moments of rest. My eyes had scarcely closed when there was a soft tap at the door. I looked down to see a woman in a fur coat, standing beside my door. I rolled the window down.

"Can I help you?"

"Would you like some company?"

"I am sorry, no. I don't buy my company."

"Alright. Could I sit in your truck for a few minutes? I am so frozen! I believe everyone else is asleep. Please? I won't be a problem!"

"Ah, okay, for a few minutes. Go around." I snapped the door lock up.

She climbed into cab and sat in the passenger seat.

"Oh my God! This feels so good! I was about to go home when I saw you drive in. I thought, why not?"

I looked at her. A black girl, but certainly as many white attributes as well as black. Pretty. Something exotic about her. Tall, maybe six foot, slender but not skinny. She wore a knee length fur coat with a hood that crumpled on her shoulders. When she turned, her hood fell off her hair. Her hair was dark, but with a reddish tint. The coat fell open. She was wearing only bikini underwear, and nothing on top. I was speechless. She was striking. Beautiful breasts, flawless skin, great legs, small waist, beautiful hips. She could have been a Playboy model.

"You know, I must disagree with your statement about not paying for your companionship. To some degree, that is most usually not true. You know it is a Yin and Yang Universe, the positive, the negative, always a pay and obtain, nothing is free. If you want food, you must obtain it and prepare it, or pay someone else to do it. Husbands and wives are on a prostitute and john basis. The pay is just different. You go into a restaurant and ask for food, the lady brings you food. Is she a whore, too? She just provided you with a necessity. Sex is a necessity. There is little difference, only in the eye of the beholder."

Her voice and elocution were well delivered. She spoke well, and she had an air of authority about her. She was in charge of her own mind. She delivered her message well as any business woman in any office in downtown Chicago would.

"So, young lady, are you an attorney for a day job and you only do this at night cause you have insomnia?" I laughed.

She laughed as well, a light, happy laugh.

"Well, I just believe people should keep things in the proper perspective, that's all."

She stuck her chin out in playful defiance and smiled.

"Ok, tell me this. How about people that really love one person, and have no desire for anyone else? Is that still give and take, or is it just becoming one?"

"For some, there is that. And people are on a sliding scale of how much they will look to others to supply their needs, and for this there must be a way to pay for it."

"Ok, I am one of those guys that only really sees one woman at a time."

"I understand. But, you know, I can have sex with three or four guys a night if I like them, and stare into each of their faces, and revel in their manliness, and enjoy every moment as we fuck each other silly. I don't do it every night. I have had good jobs in the corporate world. I realized one day that more time was spent with the men around me, checking out my body, then was spent in honest conversation about business. I noticed this more and more. Then, one day we had a motivational speaker come to hold meeting for sales. At one point in his talk he said fully half of all businesses spend most their time selling something that is often not needed or hard to sell. Think about it. What a success you would be if you had class A product to sell, that almost all thought was most desirable.

"I swear, I felt like he looked right at me! But regardless, he seemed to speak right to me. I went home that night in deep thought. Now, I have learned a little in life. I always got high grades in school. I was aware of the whore stigma, and if it was to visible, the bad effects on my life it could have. I walked into my room. A boyfriend had left a porn movie. I played it on my TV, and I watched while the girls did everything they did on the whole video. I was about half disgusted when I was through. I took all my clothes off. I checked every perspective, every angle. I thought to myself, 'I look every bit as good as any of those girls, and better than most of them!' I knew how to do all the things they did to all those guys, and to the girls. But, here again, it is perspective. All of a sudden, I had a whole new outlook on sex. I couldn't wait to try it out! It was midnight. I remembered earlier I had seen the maintenance guy the apartment kept on call at their office. I called him and gave him my room number I told him I needed him for a couple of minutes. When he arrived, I was in my bedroom. He knocked, I buzzed the door to open.

"Now, this guy was maybe 42 or so, nice looking, kinda wiry. Looked like Sam Elliott. I had put on a sexy pair of underwear and a good looking bra. He walked in. As he did, I came out of the bedroom. I walked around him and just nudged him back onto the couch. He sat down.

"I said, 'I need your services for a few moments, just relax.' I knelt on the floor and opened his trousers. I reached inside and extracted quite a substantial penis, which was growing even larger by the moment. As I stood it up, I watched it in awe, like a marvelous statue that I was about to finish. I purred to it and praised it, then I licked it. Then more, until finally I took it all in my mouth, making sounds as if I had found the most extraordinary gourmet treat that had ever been. I kept it as far back in my throat as I could, while working with my fingers and tongue. He lifted me almost straight up and exploded.

"I realized from that moment on, that if you enjoy what you do, and take it as creating a beautiful piece of art, it will be just that. And that includes sex as well.

"My apartment was always well maintained after that, and it got all the extras!

"So, there you go. For a while I kept my job for sometime. I did discretely find a few ways to use my new technique to make that job easier. And, oh yeah, the conventions rocked after that. I never asked for money, I always let the trade be suggested. Pretty soon though, it became too confining. I suppose I became what most would call a high dollar escort. I didn't look at it that way, I just had a popular dating schedule. And I never asked for money."

254

"So what are you doing here? This is a long way from the high dollar escort world."

"Well, my car is over there, in the lot. It won't run. I did go to the restaurant, but I didn't like the vibes.

"So, that is when I found you."

"And this is the way you dress all time?"

"Not all time. The coat would be too hot for summer," she smiled.

"I am what I sell, and I try to package and market myself attractively. But I didn't intend to get trapped in this snowstorm, either. But I am glad I did now."

We talked for several hours. I finally said, "I am tired. If you wish, you may come back and lay down with me though."

We went back to the bunk, and I lay down with my back next to the wall. She backed into the bunk in front of me. I put my arm around her. We lay there for a few minutes, then she said, "Aw, this is so good! Thank you so much!"

I awoke with day light coming through the bunk curtain. She rolled over and looked up at me. She raised her body up and kissed me on the cheek.

"This has been a pleasure, my friend. Are you sure there is nothing I can do for you?"

"You did. You gave me some really good material for a book I am writing. And then there was the pleasure of your company. And also, sleeping with you and feeling you close to me was very satisfying. You are not bad to look at either."

"Well, then, thank you as well. It was a morning well spent, and amply rewarding. I am going to go call AAA, and get them to tow me to a shop."

With that she stepped out of my life and disappeared, as quickly as she appeared a few hours earlier.

I never even knew her name. She made a lasting impression on me though. I'll never forget her.

As the tow truck exited the parking lot a little later with the late model Caddie on it's hook, and a striking passenger riding shotgun, I couldn't help wondering if she would be charged for the tow.

I came away with the thought, though, that if people would put the energy and focus and dedication into their relationships as they do into their careers, maybe there would be more happy people.

Then I thought of Cat. Did either of us really try? I slipped the tranny into second and slowly eased out of the snowy lot. Earlier, it held an almost surreal setting, now it was just old buildings, melting snow, and the busyness of an industrial city waking up to a cold winter's day.

I headed south on I-55. Even St. Louis would be warmer that the Windy.

There is a saying "whenever you are ready, a teacher will appear." I felt last night I had a life lesson revealed to me.

May, 1987. I am sitting in a truck stop in Indio, California. The dust is blowing hard all the way to

Banning. It was better to get off the road and shut it all down for a while. So Sheryl and I have a nice table in a sunny window. I am writing in my book. I have two or three notepads and my tape recorder scattered about. On the other side, Sheryl is drawing little pictures of trucks and bikes and people. It is a quiet Sunday afternoon in Southern California.

A voice asked, "What are you writing? Looks like a big project."

I look up. A man in his 40's or early 50's was standing looking over my shoulder. He is dressed in a Polo shirt, and shorts, and has an air of success about him. Definitely a California type.

"Oh, it is a book about truck driving, and stories from the road that I have seen and been told, and how I fell into the business."

"Could I read couple of pages?"

"Sure. I'll warn you, though, I am no professional writer. It might be a bit crude."

He picked up a note pad and read a couple of pages. Then he laid it down, and picked another and thumbed through it. He spent about 15 or 20 minutes reading my stories. He finally stopped.

"What are you going to name your book?"

"I, well.... I have thought about calling it *White Lines and Lot Lizards*."

He through back his head and laughed. "By all means, do it! That's priceless. It will sell on name value alone." He turned for the first time to Sheryl.

"Is this your illustrator?"

I looked at Sheryl. She smiled slightly.

"Yeah, that's what she is, and more. She is also my co-driver and partner."

"Sheryl, how long have you been driving?"

"About 15 years."

"And you, sir, how long?"

"About 17."

"That is inspiring. You two are remarkable to display the talents you do, in a world I wasn't expecting it from."

"Thought all truckers were dumb, huh?"

"I never thought much of them in any respect. They were just always there, a part of the furniture so to speak. Your writing is a revelation. You are very good, you know.

"I want you to take my card. When you are finished with this, I would like to get first choice on it. I am a partner in a publishing firm. I think it is a winner. Please, do I get that opportunity?"

"I, well.... sure, why not? If you like it, then sure!"

He handed me his card. Very fancy. I was a bit shy when I took my card out and gave it to him.

"My goodness, a truck driver with a card! Mr. Evan Smith, you never cease to amaze me! I would like to know more about your world. I think everyone would."

"So, would you like to go see our house and our ride, Mr. Derek?"

"Oh yes, of course I would."

The wind had dropped by now. I walked him out to the Pete. I opened the driver's door and told him to climb up. I walked to the passenger side, opened the door and climbed up. He sat with both hands on the wheel, and bounced a bit in the air seat.

"This thing has more gauges than my sports car! Amazing, Evan, and it is so attractively finished inside. I really like this!"

Shortly, Sheryl came out and we sat and told him trucking stories till almost dark. Robert Derek went away that evening in a whole different state of mind. Oh, did I mention we smoked some really good weed with him as well?

Well, after that I thought maybe this was going to make the story more important. But no. I realized, the importance of the story was in the telling, not by chance it might get to be a big hit. It only had to be a big hit in my mind.

I decided I was going to start paying more attention to the important places in the country where we visited, and be better able to describe them. I would put maybe just a little more effort to it.

Life is good, if you make it that way. So much of it I spent chasing the ghosts that drive most men. We are such simple creatures. We claim to be so evolved, yet the same forces still drive us that drove ancient man. The desire for property, or possessions. The desire to breed - sometimes that is the one that holds us back from achievements. We get so focused on it, we can think of little else. I saw much of this in the truck stops around the country. It was the obsession of the evening, to get laid, or at least a blow job.

Another thing that holds people back from achieving is the obsession of forgetting their reality. This usually comes from drinking or drugs.

Sometimes drugs are as casual as cigarettes or coffee. Did you ever hear people say, 'Oh, I just can't get started without my cup of coffee!' Why? What magical thing does coffee have to make you be able to get up and move? None, is the answer.

Or, how about, 'I can't quit smoking!' Really? There are millions of people out there that don't drink coffee, or smoke, and many of them surpass your sorry ass in achievement even with your little vices you can't do with out.

I knew a man that had a business that hired workers. He called cigarettes "One Armed Bandits." He said they would steal 25 % of the work productivity from him everyday, and on top of that, he would be forced to smell the nasty stuff.

Ok, you get my point. But I had been very lucky. Our business was thriving. I had set up the business on a plan that after a year each employee received a share of the profit. Every year the share got larger. We had a few that weren't slated for this, but they passed on to other endeavors.

When the Gulf War broke out in August of 1991, we immediately got a huge rush of business. That continued through the winter, and even on after it was over in February. I was sorry to see another war, but I marveled at the advances in technology since Vietnam. I'll bet some of those old Korean and WWII vets that were still living were just shocked.

My good friend and partner, Sheryl, we are still driving and sharing life on the road. We had purchased a new truck in '91, with an apartment sized sleeper. We specialized in loads that required sometimes long waits - government stuff and corporate hauls. We have a generator that we could run that powers our apartment with a refrigerator. We have fresh water tanks and waste water tanks, like the big RV's do.

We began to take the opportunity to go to National Parks and see America. Wherever we go, people are curious about the large car that carries us around the country. We sometimes allow people a short tour, especially children. We always tell them how the needs of America are carried on the backs of the American Trucker. How many miles they drove per week or year, and all the details that we can that will promote a good image.

By the mid 90's, I decided to take more time off

the road. I spent considerable time writing. I became involved with some veteran groups. Our business took care of itself, or rather, all of us together took care of it. It had never been a burden. I sometimes thought Frenchy was still up there somewhere watching over us.

I still keep in touch with all my friends from Vietnam, and the many I have met in the trucking world. I correspond with Cat these days. Oh, yeah, she got married, had a couple of kids and still lives in California. Her son is a truck driver, and her daughter is a nurse. And, she is about to be a Grandma! Imagine, beautiful Cat, a grandma! But that is what happens in life. It is a circle that is passed down. Yeah, and I am in my 60's now. Hard to believe. I have not yet given up my desire for the open road. Most of the time I satisfy it from the seat of our RV. I still sometimes feel the need to sit in a big truck stop and listen to the BS on the CB radio. I love America, I love it's sights, it's history, it's freedom. I still look with wonder down the white lines with the same eyes I used in 1970. I am still housed in the same body. Yeah, the body has changed, but most do. Would I go back and do those miles over again? Oh, Hell, Yes! I would! I wouldn't miss any of it, not a single mile. I wouldn't want to miss a single conversation, or miss a single tall story, or not meet anyone of those brothers of the highway, or sisters of the road, that became friends over the years. Because of each of them, I have learned to be the happy, satisfied, content person that I am today. They made me, those experiences shaped me, the hardships refined me. The friendships calmed me. My time was well spent. The mystery at the end of the white lines kept me going. And I learned acceptance of all around me; from the drivers, the waitresses, all the people in all the truck stops in America, the dockworkers in Jersey, the construction workers everywhere. Oh, yes, and we can't forget about the lot lizards. They are apart of the lifestyle as well. That is what it is all about.

White lines and lot lizards.

Epilogue

Evan, had he been a real person, and I hesitate to say that he wasn't, he was very real to me. I think he would have retired a happy and successful man. Many of the Vietnam Vets have achieved that comfort in their lives. When most of us, barely out of high school, found ourselves in an exotic foreign land, living with people much different than ourselves, often in life and death situations, it changed us.

It took those traits we learned from our parents and teachers, and subjected them to closer scrutiny and placed them in stressful situations. Most of us had to learn to adapt, but still, we were changed. Upon release from that accelerated lifestyle, and all that was contained in it, we were told to go home and resume our former life, and just forget what had just happened. For many, that was difficult, for some, impossible. So we came home and created new lifestyles, a blend of the former and the latter. But our coloring books seemed to look just a bit different than the norm. Some of us just couldn't seem to not color outside the lines.